Taming the Boiling Pot

Turning Down the Heat
in Times of Conflict and Crisis

CLIFF COUCH

Scripture references marked NIV are from the HOLY BIBLE, NEW INTERNATIONAL VERSION. Copyright © 1973, 1978, 1984 International Bible Society. Used by permission of Zondervan Bible Publishers.

Scripture references marked NASB are taken from the NEW AMERICAN STANDARD BIBLE®, Copyright © 1960, 1962, 1963, 1968, 1971, 1972, 1973, 1975, 1977, 1995 by the Lockman Foundation. Used by permission.

Scripture quotations marked (NLT) are taken from the Holy Bible, New Living Translation, copyright © 1996. Used by permission if Tyndale House Publishers, Inc., Wheaton, Illinois 60189. All rights reserved.

Scripture references marked KJV are from The King James Version of the Bible.

ISBN: 1453659552
ISBN-13: 9781453659557

Dedication

TO MARTI: The beat of our heart "has gone many miles, far into the big numbers" ("Honey and Salt," Carl Sandburg). You are my love, my fairest treasure in this life, the most excellent of all women. No matter what crisis we share, we beat as one heart, now and forever.

Acknowledgements

No man who is worth a cent would dare presume that any worthwhile work he produces is his alone. I have been blessed beyond measure by a support team whom I am privileged to acknowledge to all who may find something useful in these pages. My thanks to each of them is but a poor return for their kindness and investment in me.

Marti Couch. My beloved wife, best friend and confidant' has shared every step of this journey with me. Her professional expertise in counseling, generally, and child and adult relationship dynamics, specifically, has added insights, stories and humor to the complex web of crisis and conflict management. But her greatest contribution may well be her ability to daily manage the stresses of a home where many kids and their friends have grown up and moved on to successful maturity, a process that now continues with an adopted daughter and a new generation of 'tweens and teens.

Cliff II, Joel, Jason, Christopher, Mary, Sean and Felicity. Our children, all of whom but Felicity are grown and successful, bore with my ineptitudes as I struggled to learn how to be a dad and how to help coach them through the occasional rough spots of their own wonderful adventures. They were and are my proving ground in God's greatest theater of conflict of all: the family. Like Marti, my dear Felicity has had to put up with the erratic schedule of a first time author, whose frazzled ways she has endured with extraordinarily loving patience and great good humor.

Colin, Katy and Dr. Mike. Our beloved godchildren have spent years in our home and have blessed us with their own journeys, enriching us in ways past measuring. They, too, are a part of the overall fabric of this book.

Barry Capece. In large measure, this book would never have made it to print but for Barry's gently fierce belief that there is a message here worth proclaiming. He coached an unknown writer through to the finish line of publication, offering counsel on almost every conceivable aspect of authorship and publication while treading the fine line between friendship and editorial direction.

Pastor Eric Hulet. As this manuscript came together, Pastor Eric graciously read the first draft. His suggestions and gentle corrections made the entire book more readable, as well as Biblically accurate.

Dr. Stan Seat. He is the "friend that sticks closer than a brother" who has handled the delicate psyche of this author with diversion, burgers and good cheer on many occasions when the author's own pot was boiling over, if not cracking up all together.

Barbara Keen. A valiant prayer warrior and constant source of aid despite her own adversities, Barbara's efforts in the heavenly realms helped turn this project from dream to reality.

Carrie McCurdy. If ever a copy editor bore her author's burdens, it is here. From cleaning up rusty grammar to serving as a sounding board as this book reached critical mass, Carrie has offered technical assistance and wisdom far beyond her years.

Jay Heinlein. When a master of the publishing craft was needed, Jay took the tiller and directed the ship to port. Without him, the shoals and rocks might have claimed yet another fledgling author.

Many others have shared insights, provided suggestions and offered prayer and encouragement. I am indebted to each of you for your special, valued contributions.

And to each of you, who open your heart to me by allowing me to travel the path of conflict and crisis with you in the pages that follow, know that my prayers have been with you from the first words you are about to read. Thanks for sharing a part of your journey with me.

Contents

Introduction

LIVING WITH CONFLICT AND CRISIS

"I have told you these things, so that in Me you may have peace. In this world you will have trouble. But take heart! I have overcome the world." John 16:33, NIV

We tend to avoid that which we find to be unpleasant. Instinct has something to do with it. Were we to be placed in harsh, neo-apocalyptic conditions, our noses, without any prompting, would tell us to avoid certain water and food sources. Touch, taste, sight would all become sensitized to survival while our senses of fight or flight would alter to meet the challenges of a different local reality. Wondrously created beings that we are, Our Father has built into us the means to confront and overcome a lifetime of conflict and crisis.

He has built it into not only our genetic code but into our spiritual makeup. When confronted with the garden-variety set of daily problems, we tend to operate on emotional instinct and common sense. But that will only carry us so far. It is one thing to work our way through a stack of bills when we have a paycheck to cover them. Yet it is quite another to grapple with supporting ourselves when we are out of work and out of money. Sometimes, we must face a new personal reality, one that for us is unprecedented or seldom encountered. Our Father will show us that we have the strength to do so if we will but seek Him.

I share with you this voyage of discovery. Being in the legal business, I traffic daily in the currency of discord so I have walked the road of conflict and crisis management many times. May I first share with you my two personal greatest fears when I face a major problem? That I will have to do so alone and that I will be inadequate to the challenge. Scripture tells us that we are never alone. Even if your own parents forsake you, God will receive you (Psalm 27:10). And it is Our Father who "trains my hands for war, my fingers for battle" (Psalm 144:1, NIV) as the warrior King David rejoiced. Ergo: I am not alone and God Himself prepares me. This is just the beginning. You will see any number of issues, questions and situations addressed in the chapters that follow. And I am not afraid to speak with you about the tough stuff of life.

Our Father has the answers and He has placed them before us in His Holy Word. So as you will see, this book is top-heavy with Bible references. When I prepare a legal argument, I cite the best cases and sources I can find for the proposition at hand. The judge does not care much about what I think on a subject. He wants to know what the authorities have to say. So, too, I have given you God's authority, not my own. With the confidence of God's revealed truth and power and with the certainty that He is personally committed to your ultimate success, you can confront the trouble before you.

This book is more about relationship and life choices than it is about dry technique. You see, for the next dozen-plus chapters, we are companions, sitting around the coffee shop or talking across the bleachers at a kid ball game. Together we share as friends the struggles common to all of us. We will talk about uncertainty and about what it means when familiar landmarks and resources dry up. Our hearts will grapple with the sovereignty and grace of God and how it helps us in the day of trouble. Grief, loss, moral integrity, the struggle to hold on in life's darkest moments, the mystery of love, the glory of dreams, the finding of peace, all are fair game for us. We will see that strength for the crazy times is within our reach and before we have finished, we will even have explored the eternal partnership God wants with each of us.

To make it easier to identify key points, I have made rather frequent use of italics and headings. And the style is conversational throughout—it is how friends talk with each other, right? Once in a while I repeat myself. But that is because each chapter, basically, is intended to stand on its own. If you need some quick help with moral integrity, turn right away to *Spider Webs and Gnats*. If you are having one of those days where every pot in the kitchen is boiling over, you may get a chuckle from *When Pandemonium Reigns*. Should you find yourself in a major life crisis, go to *Permission to Downsize* and *Just a Little Longer* to receive some specific insights and tools about getting through the worst storms of life. I hope you will find some directly applicable help for your specific crisis.

Above all else, thanks for letting me visit with you. No one else could possibly be you. God knows that better than anyone and it is why He has a perfect plan for you to successfully navigate the waters of conflict and crisis.

Chapter 1

EMBRACING NEW BEGINNINGS

"In the beginning God created..." Genesis 1:1, NASB

Sunlight and moonlight frame our days and nights no differently today than they did yesterday. Yet each day, each hour, is as different as the lights of the heavens are constant. How can the tears or the joys of the moment be reconciled to the eternity of the cosmos? And where, oh where do we fit in? Or do we fit in at all?

The yearnings of the sleepless night and restless days point us to Our Father's compass. He, alone, created all. He, alone, can reset the clock of our soul.

We wanderers of cyberspace and empty-space in rooms packed with things that are only illusions of reality, constantly hear and see the world scream "new" at us. "Buy that new convertible and capture the freedom!" sums up the substance of Madison Avenue's message. New clothes. New homes. New bodies. But does anybody care? Does anybody notice? Will anybody love us anymore after the new is no longer new?

This story is not about the new that fades as quickly as the coveted new car scent. It is about new that remains new, that remains fresh and vibrant, not just now but forever.

In the Beginning, God, Not Man, Created

It is 5:00 in the morning. Let's take a short walk together. It is summertime. The earth smells richly of verdant plant life that has its roots in soil that is untold thousands of years old but is still as fresh as warm bread. Do you hear the cardinal singing from the oak tree? His melody has not changed since the week of Creation. Yet the notes we hear will never be heard again. Catch the breeze while you may, for it, too, quickly passes, only to be replaced by another of its kind. Touch a flower. That texture is exactly as God made it on the third day. You see, Our Father's Creation is *timeless*. And so are you because He made you in His own image, no less so than the delightful creations by which we are blessed in our short stroll together.

Where His Feet pass, all is new. Embrace His perfect newness in this moment to begin your own new day. That is your first step. And the second is equally simple. Accept His plan that you become new, no matter what has happened to you or where you are at this moment in your journey.

In the caterpillar existence of an incomplete, troubled soul, we yearn for the butterfly's sweetness of release. How, then, do we become "new"? Go to Our Father. His arms are open to embrace you, no matter what your perceived shortcomings or wrongdoings. The Ancient of Days wants you, yearns for you and keeps the light of His heavenly home ever burning for you. When home is no longer home, recall the words of Moses: "Lord, you have been our dwelling place in all generations…from everlasting to everlasting you are God" (Psalm 90: 1-2, NASB).

You are no less desirable to Our Father because you are a bundle of problems. Consider the work of the artist who makes mosaics. He takes broken, seemingly useless pieces of tile, glass or other materials and creates from them a new, stunning masterpiece. And why, dear one, can't you be His next great work? Does the shame of your misdeeds keep you from His Workshop? Or do you fear the touch of His Hands? He who perfectly created all things continually works in the ordinary miracles of human process. Where He applies the chisel, He also applies the gentle lubricant of compassion, expressed in the kindness of others whom He places in our path.

So, where do we begin?

What Our Father Has Done Before, He Will Do Again

When we accept the hope of new beginnings, we embrace not our strength but His. We will use this as a Northstar reference point many times in these pages. When you drive your car, truck or SUV, you rely on the collective experience of untold millions of hours of automotive engineering and manufacturing history. We seldom if ever stop to think about it. We turn the key and off we fly to our next destination. It's no big deal. The strength of others enlarges our own abilities and we accept it as an ordinary part of life.

Carry the analogy upward to the heavenly realms, taking the story of Abraham as an example. God told Abraham and Sarah they would be changing diapers and chasing a toddler when most folks their age would be napping on the front porch. Many centuries later, Our Father announced that His Son's forerunner would be born to yet another couple well past the usual child-rearing years. Imagine the celebration when Elizabeth gave birth to the boy child who would grow up to become John the Baptist! So it is that Our Father's strength becomes our strength when we allow Him to work.

This is a principle of both His faithfulness and His replication. From science, we have learned that if the results of a study are accurate and truthful, they can be re-produced by another scientist using the same methodology. The orderliness of Our Father's Creation points to His consistency. Take to heart Our Father's promise, "Never will I leave you; never will I forsake you" (Hebrews 13:5, NIV). What He has done for others, He will also do for you, according to His perfect plan for you. He will do it flawlessly, time after time after time. Let me repeat this crucial point: *what Our Father has done before, He will do again, for He is faithful in all things.* You may not even be aware that danger lurks down the street when He has already prepared a protection for you. Let me share a story to prove the point.

During the 1990s, when I was a 40-something-age runner, I was a fairly good local competitor at the five kilometer (3.1 mile) distance. During the terribly hot Dallas summer of 1998, I trained most mornings beginning around 4:45 a.m. when the air had cooled down to a frosty 82 degrees or so. One such morning, I was running along a major street when I heard footsteps running behind me. That was unusual so I kicked the pace up a notch. About that time, I heard someone yell, "You are never gonna catch that dude! He's way too fast for you!" I chuckled a bit and thought to myself, "He doesn't have a clue how fast this dude can *really* run!" Then, I started sprinting at a pace that the local high school cross country team would have found impressive. That was the end of the race.

When I finally slowed down nearly a mile later, I was thinking of how all my running trophies and medals seemed pretty insignificant for I had just won the one race that mattered. But I was not quite finished. As I approached the next major intersection, an attractive young lady ran past me, headphones and all, down the exact way from which I had just escaped. Holding up my hands, I warned her of what had just happened to me. Wisely, she headed back to her apartment while I took a different way home.

What for me was a rather amusing war story to share with my running friends, for her could have been life and death. And that is how Our Father works. In the whirl of unforeseen circumstances, He is already there, preparing a way.

Growing Up God's Kids

Go back to a time when you were a kid. Anytime in the past few minutes will suffice because we are still and always will be God's kids, no matter how old we are. How do you raise your children? Perhaps you are one of the millions of parents who have taken to heart this Bible verse: "Train up a child in the way he should go, Even when he is old he will not depart from it" (Proverbs 22:6, NASB). Our Father, too, raises all His children in the way they should go. Stop for a moment and place the emphasis on the word "he" in the first part of that last verse. It now reads like this: "Train up a child in the way *he* should go…" Not only does Our Father lead you "in the paths of righteousness for His name's sake" (Psalm 23:3, KJV) but He also has a lifelong plan to raise you in a very specific way. *Our Father uses conflict and crisis to help raise you in the way He wants you to go.*

Look upon conflict and crisis as a process, one that ebbs and flows throughout a lifetime. When you run clothes through the washing machine, you let all the cycles finish before removing them. God is no different. In His grand eternal plan, He causes or allows you to interact with a certain amount of agitation, no different than our washing machine example. Agitation cleans us up and makes us ready for our next use, in a manner of speaking, if we let Him have His way with us. Through Scripture, He instructs us, filling us with knowledge. By helping us to understand His holy perspective, He increases our wisdom. He gives us understanding through experience that we gain in applying His knowledge with wisdom to numerous life events (Colossians 1:9), many of which are conflictual in nature. Through it all, like Morning Glories on a spring trellis, He continually trains us up ever higher in the way we should go until life here becomes life hereafter for each of us.

"New" Means "Blessed," Not Barren

Perhaps you do some gardening from time to time. If so, you know the joy of watching a springtime flower bed come to life again. One day, all is brown and lifeless. Then the little miracle happens. First one shoot, then another, then many others sound the clarion call of a new gardening year.

Life begins again in many ways. We have known new school years and new jobs, new loves, new dwellings and new adventures. Perhaps your garden is a kitchen where you retreat, as one acquaintance of mine does when he is troubled, to create something pleasant. Or maybe it is a workbench or a basketball court or a sewing basket or a craft area. Beginning something new calms us, centers us and allows us to feel the stirrings of life's deeper currents when the rush and heat of the daily grind causes us to seek shade.

We remember not the empty blackboard but the equation solved, the song sung, the promise fulfilled. *Just as fire clears the undergrowth of a forest, adversity prepares us for change.* What lies under the soot of apparent desolation is the silent promise of new seed, needing only a little sunlight and water to explode into a symphony of glory.

New beginnings can be both challenging and riotously chaotic and fun at the same time. When Marti and I returned from our honeymoon on Christmas night, we came into a household of four high school and college-aged kids who had not been fed and who could not wait a minute for their Christmas with us. So, grabbing one of the kids, I headed for the 'fridge to start a very late dinner while Marti put Christmas together. It was definitely not the quiet homecoming she had planned for me on our first night home together with the kids. But Oh! What a crazy, great time we had! A hurried dinner at 11:00 p.m. led quickly into torn Christmas wrappings, barking dogs and an appearance by Fred the giant iguana lizard. When the decibel level settled, at last, below 100, our daughter looked up at us and said "This was the best Christmas ever!" In bed around 2:00 a.m., Marti quietly laughed and said "Welcome home, dad!"

Welcome home, indeed. For the blessed happiness of new beginnings lies only a prayer and a wildly delightful moment away.

Chapter 2

WHEN THE BROOK DRIES UP

"Then the word of the LORD came to Elijah: 'Leave here, turn eastward and hide in the Kerith Ravine, east of the Jordan. You will drink from the brook, and I have ordered the ravens to feed you there.' So he did what the LORD told him...Sometime later the brook dried up...Then the word of the Lord came to him: 'Go at once to Zarephath of Sidon and stay there." 1 Kings 17:2-5, 7-9, NIV

At one time or another you have likely engaged in the fascinating challenge of piecing together a jigsaw puzzle. Perhaps it was with family or maybe you were simply bored one rainy day as you dusted off the box with the colorful picture, opened it and poured all the pieces on the table. As that pile of hundreds of cut-out segments lay before you, what thought dominated your mind? Was it "How will I ever get this thing together?" (my response, by the way) or "I can't wait to get started!"

And so you began to lay the pieces out, turning them right-side up as you searched for the border pieces, from which you moved to different segments of the picture. You probably looked at the box quite often for guidance. Gradually, oh so slowly at first, the pieces looked a little less disorganized. Then shapes and sequences began to appear as you started seeing combinations emerge. Like a true puzzle-master, you did not quit, even though you walked away from time to time. When you left the table I suspect you did not totally abandon the project. Even while you were away, subconsciously or consciously you worked at solving the puzzle. When you came back, you looked at the picture differently. Sometimes a portion of the picture just would not come into focus. What did you do? You tried another part of the puzzle, walked around the table to see it from a different angle, took a break, got help from someone else or maybe you simply let it go for the time being.

Life's puzzle plays out the same way. Sometimes we stick with it. Sometimes we let go and move on. Both approaches have their place for they are each different sides of the same spiritual coin. *Letting go does not mean giving up. It means seeing God's Hand move us in a different direction when He dries up the brook.* Let's team up and see if we can fit this one together.

Wearing Out Our Welcome

We lead our bodies on a merry chase, don't we? Staying up too late then getting up too early, only to stuff them full of calories, cholesterol and caffeine, we subject our mortal members to stress tests that even the most modern of army battle tanks could scarcely hope to handle. Even those nine-life cats know better than to do some of the crazy stuff we do. Mea maxima culpa. I am *very* guilty. I prefer not to admit that I am over 30, over 40, over 50, soon to be going once, going twice and gone like some junk-store reject at a flea market auction.

At some point, we will all wear out our welcome with different pieces of our physical puzzle. Letting go goes with the territory. Learning how to gracefully let go will help us land on our feet and may just inspire those around us, as Lois (not her real name) inspired me when I was a kid.

Lois was born without arms. Try telling her it was a handicap and you might just have gotten a well-aimed rock in your side! Boy, could she throw! Goliath would have run from her as she grabbed a stone with her toes and hurled it with unerring accuracy and seemingly ballistic force at whatever she chose. She could paint, catch grasshoppers, fish and do the whole host of daily small tasks we take for granted. Lois let go of her arms, preferring not to use prosthetics. I suspect they would have hindered the embrace she had on life.

Our love of the gift of physical capability compels us to examine not just our waistline but the weightier matter of outlook. OK, so I can't run with the top dogs anymore. I can still walk the dogs under my own power. And I bet that when you cannot walk as far as you like, you can still get around either with the help of a walker, a friend or a wheel chair. If we can be mobile, we still have much for which to be thankful. On it goes. If we cannot see, hear or think as clearly, go as far or jump as high as we once did, we can compensate in other ways. As we have heard it said, life looks pretty good if we can still smell the daisies and not just their roots.

But what of the problems of our younger days? How do we reconcile the issues of classroom stresses, dating, courtship and relationship uncertainties, burdened bank statements, growing families, nano-second business demands, substance abuse & sexual temptations with the need to keep our mental, as well as our physical balance? If there is anything close to a universal answer, it rests in Our Father's concept of life's seasons.

Just as there is a season for advanced age, there is also a season for youth and for middle-age. We learn every day how to be who and what we are in the moment. As time passes, we can choose to be a preschooler again while enjoying the trucks and blocks that mark the playroom adventures of a three-year-old son. When that three-year-old is thirty years old, we can again experience life with him wherever he finds himself, for we have been there before. *Living life's seasons fully helps us to help others live them successfully.* In days gone by, some large hospitals had a see-one, do-one, teach-one system as to medical procedures for young physicians. I wonder if Our Father sometimes approaches life that way with us. Could it just be that the thing that troubles me today may be that which I will be called upon to assist another in handling on some unexpected occasion?

We rebel against the loss of vitality, be it physical, emotional or spiritual. The spark of life and personality defines who we are. When seasons change, we must wisely discern how to adjust to new surroundings without losing the essence of our makeup, avoiding thereby the snare of foreclosing life. How do we foreclose life? By engaging in destructive practices, whether they be relationship cutoff, substance abuse, workaholism or the host of practices and thought processes that may lead to seriously abnormal behaviors. "Above all else, guard your heart" said Solomon, "for it is the wellspring of life" (Proverbs 4:3, NIV). What a person harbors in his heart, he will become. Therefore, as Paul said, think on those things that are true, noble, right, pure, lovely, admirable and praiseworthy (Philippians 4:8, NIV). Heart-healthy living begins with these.

At some point, Our Father will likely dry up the brook of our physical capabilities. When that happens, we are decidedly *not* reduced to a state of mere memories. He will move us forward to our next destination for the activity He has prepared for us. Chuckle as you recall the story of the death of the prophet Elisha in 2 Kings 13:20-22 who even when he was dead still was used by God to raise to life a corpse that was thrown into Elisha's tomb. Now *there* was an encore! And you probably have quite a few encores left in you no matter what those tacky birthday cards say every year.

Loving Enough to Let Go

Sometimes the brook dries up in other ways. A cherished friend or even a spouse may desert us or a relationship with a family member or trusted colleague may sour beyond repair. What today we think of as "always" is not always that which will be.

Letting go of those we love hurts oh, so much. But sometimes it is the single kindest thing we can do. All of us must journey in our own way. For a season, we travel through a given countryside with certain companions. Then the landscape changes. New people enter our lives as others depart from it. As one wise man said, we should always remember that we are only visitors in other people's lives. When we hold the hands and hearts of others, we know the here and now of it. Only Our Father can reconcile the passing of times and loves through our tiny window into the vast eternity of His future, a future that includes the working out of all that is best for all of us.

I do not pretend to understand it. It is one thing to lose a cherished object. We may even seek it and rejoice with others when we re-discover that which was lost, as did the woman who lost an important sum of money (Luke 15:8-10). But why do relationships fall apart, like the junkyard creation of some crazed tinkerer, even when we try our best to keep them together? No, no one can entirely answer that question, despite the best efforts of those who specialize in and write about such things. The uniqueness of each relationship dictates its own dynamic. Place six identical bushes in the same garden and you will likely find differences in how or whether they grow and prosper. Cultivate six relationships with tender loving care and not all of them will necessarily bear fruit for a lifetime.

Our own imperfections and those of others cause the vehicle of relationship to suffer many mishaps. Even with the best of professional help, sometimes we must let go of one that cannot be sustained any longer. *But if we have loved, however imperfectly, we can also love enough to let others move on in their own journey, without bitterness or folly.* And in that process, we may avoid burning a bridge that someday may re-open.

By grace, many broken relationships do heal but often they change into something different. Our children grow up, perhaps adopting lifestyles or ideals that differ rather dramatically from our own. Maybe a dear friend moves many miles away or a church, sports or work acquaintance moves away from the common ground which we have shared with them. When we love enough, we accept the change and seek a new pathway where the old one has ended. By letting go of old ways and expectations, we renew the soil of our soul and theirs, allowing thereby new growth to begin, instead of interjecting the poison of relationship cutoff.

Our Father has not cut us off from Himself, even when we were and are at our worst. Nor does He expect from us what He Himself will not do. "But God demonstrates His own love toward us, in that while we were yet sinners, Christ died for us" (Romans 5:8, NASB). If we have difficulty letting go of our frustrations, our disappointments and our anxieties, recall a certain day on a Hill of Death outside of Jerusalem when darkness covered the city, for on that day, Our Loving Father let go of His Only Begotten Son so that he could catch us in mid-fall to save us from eternal destruction. And so it is that when we love Him enough to let go of that which means so much to us, Our Father will honor our trust and not allow us to be dashed to bits on the rocks below.

Why Must the Brook Dry Up?

He Who Is All Wisdom would not leave us ignorant of His ways. That is why Our Father instructs us through Scripture and leads us in such a fashion that each of us will personally understand His unique, perfect direction for each unique one of us. The brook dries up for all of us, however, for certain common reasons.

Our Father dries up the brook to focus our attention on some issue of error in our life. Sometimes I walk out into my garden and I see the remains of a flower I have trodden underfoot. Or I will notice a patch of dead grass where the bugs are eating away at the roots. On occasion, a large weed, a thorny vine or a stalk of poison ivy invades my yard and I am not aggressive enough in rooting it out. It takes over and at some point I must take stern steps to keep it from overpowering that which I have planted. The garden of my own life is no different. The poet said it well: "These clumsy feet, still in the mire, Go crushing blossoms without end; These hard, well-meaning hands, we thrust among the heart-strings of a friend" ("The Fool's Prayer," Edward R. Sill).

When we carelessly or intentionally hurt that which God cherishes, He will remind us that all living things must be nurtured. If we do not do His bidding, we will see holes in the fabric of our life where the moths have eaten through it. We are then faced with the choice of accepting Our Father's counsel and instruction to re-plant and re-weave or to accept the consequences of failing to clean up the dirty spot. Either way, the brook cannot flow again until we deal head-on with the obstacle which has slowed or stopped its flow.

Our Father dries up the brook to bring us back to Him. Sometimes our restlessness causes us to go far away into a world that seems exciting at the time. The Prodigal Son (John 15:11-31) took a direction that his father did not approve but nonetheless allowed. Our Father works the same way. Occasionally, we take a wrong turn and end up in a fast lane that empties our gas tank and our wallet, leaving us stranded by the side of a road far from home. In the moment of desolation, we recall the peaceful places of better days.

Hearing in our mind's inner ear the true call of Him who is the Lover of Our Soul, we can abandon the old jalopy knowing that it no longer matters *how* we go home or what we may look like when we arrive. All that matters is that we *go*. Our Father's front porch light never goes out. He never sleeps. He never ceases to wait for us to appear over the horizon. He cares not that we are empty-handed and smelling of pigs. *Never doubt that Our Father will rush to greet you the moment you turn to Him.* Living Water, eternally fresh, awaits you at Home.

Our Father dries up the brook to prepare us for new opportunities and direction. The nomadic tribes of the earth have always known the importance of following the water and the food supply. Cybernetic man still must do the same. So Our Father will dry up a career opportunity, a bank account, a relationship or some other source of water in order that He may force us to move on to a new pasture.

Note carefully that sometimes God dries up the brook when we are doing great works of which He approves and directs. The Apostle Paul, while in the midst of a missionary journey to plant the word of God, was directly stopped by the Holy Spirit and the Spirit of Jesus from entering the new missionary field of Asia. Acts, chapter 16: 6-15 records the story of how Paul, instead, turned west to the port city Troas where he received a vision to enter Macedonia. We know it today as Europe. By recognizing the dry brook, Paul allowed himself to be moved to a place that Our Father deemed more important at the moment. When we accept His counsel, acknowledging Him in all our ways, He will always direct our paths (Proverbs 3:5-6). By drying up the brook, Our Father allows us to pass over to new places that otherwise would be inaccessible. And we do so without even getting our feet wet.

Our Father dries up the brook to give us rest. This one hurts for I do not accept inactivity easily. I like to think I am always at my best when I am always on the go. Dad used to tell me, "Cliff, slow down!" And I would reply, "Dad, I am a Thoroughbred. I was born to race." But life is a marathon and not a 100 meter dash. We cannot sprint all the time at top speed and expect to be effective for the long haul.

God gives us rest and peace as a gift. Consider His instruction to "ask where the good way is, and walk in it, and you will find rest for your souls" (Jeremiah 6:16, NIV). It is by Our Father's own hand that we may "lie down in peace and sleep, for you alone, O LORD, make me dwell in safety" (Psalm 4:8, NIV). Perhaps no other words comfort us like those of Jesus who said, "Come to me, all you who are weary and burdened, and I will give you rest" (Matthew 11:28, NIV). When the flow of the brook slows down, sometimes Our Father desires that we slow down with it to enjoy the peaceful, lazy summer days of refreshment that He has provided.

A Moment for Grief, A Lifetime for Joy

We may wonder if Elijah was sad when he learned that his peaceful place in the valley with the flowing brook was no longer to be his home. At one time or another, all of us have felt the tugging on our heart when we left a special home, vacation retreat or the sheltered abode of a friend or family member. Our Father gives us the gift of memory to help us retain that which has passed before us. Many times, I have recalled the verse of the English poet, Algernon Swinburn who said that *"time remembered is grief forgotten."*

When you find yourself at a place where the brook is drying up, it is OK to be sad. But only remain sad for a comparative moment. As David wrote in Psalm 30:5 (NASB) "Weeping may last for the night, But a shout of joy comes in the morning." Morning *will* come. The sky will clear, the flowers will reopen and the brook will begin to flow again, carrying you ever forward to new adventures.

Chapter 3

PERMISSION TO DOWNSIZE

"There is an appointed time for everything.
And there is a time for every event under heaven...
A time to throw stones and a time to gather stones."
Ecclesiastes 3:1, 5, NASB

This chapter is about casting away stones either because it is forced upon us or because we must do so to improve our circumstances. Let us begin with a hard admission: downsizing hurts, plain and simple. When we face that timeless fear of loss, we shrink from both its process and its end result. We would generally prefer to acquire than to eliminate. My waistline bears testimony to this truth. I can pack on pounds with ease but taking them off calls for pain before I see the gain.

We are all veterans of downsizing. Even if we face new obstacles, they are still only stones to be moved, nothing more and nothing less. If we step on a stone we may receive a stone bruise but the stone stays in place even as we move on. Similarly, our possessions fall away but we move ever forward. The trick is to minimize the damage from the stones we leave behind. Let me share a story with you.

I am both sentimental and a packrat. It sometimes is a messy, frustrating combination. When it came time for us to move to a much smaller home a while back, I frankly was overwhelmed by the task of which stones to cast away and which ones to keep. Solomon's wisdom did not help much. I knew it was time to downsize. But my heart just was not into it.

You of course understand the problem. My feelings of attachment to things that had personal history stood squarely in the path of Our Father's new direction for Marti and me. I knew we needed to be in a smaller home now that the kids were grown. I knew with great certainty that He had guided us to a wonderful new, special place. Still, it hurt to think of letting go of stuff, with all its personal history and meaning, which had been around for such a long time.

Pardon the pun, but Marti had to knock some of the "stuff"–ing out of me. "Honey," she tried to reason, "we are dropping a thousand square feet of living space *and* moving from a three car garage to a small two car garage. You have to get rid of some things or we will be living on top of your junk!" "Yeah, yeah, yeah, I know," I responded. So off I went to the garage to start the task. You would have thought I was going to a funeral. In a sense I *was* going to a funeral for I was experiencing feelings of grief over loss. Objectively, I understood that much of what was in those boxes could not be that important if I had not even bothered to pull them down from the shelf in years. So opening them one at a time, I began to do what had to be done.

I enjoyed the old running shirts, worn out books and stray papers one last time. I even allowed myself to be a little sad as I sorted out what I really wanted to repack and move versus what I was willing to give away or throw away.

Strangely, it got easier after the first few minutes. It was as if I began to grasp the idea that I was not being disloyal to the people and events with which I connected those old souvenirs of by-gone times. I did not need "things" to make me whole and happy. By getting rid of the clutter, I was focusing myself on what really mattered, clarifying my values and perspective at the same time. The "get rid of" stack slowly became larger than the "keep it" pile. By the time the day was over, I had downsized in respectable fashion and I had developed a newfound strength, even a certain enjoyment, for letting go and moving on. That is what the process of healthy downsizing is about.

It is no easier to downsize than it is possible to avoid it. Yet Our Father has His reasons for occasionally clearing out our physical, emotional and spiritual garage. He gives us both permission and instruction to downsize. Following His lead draws us away from the junk and toward what matters to Him. Sometimes the journey has a sentimental edge to it that is both sweet and bitter. At other times our road to downsizing takes us through the deepest of valleys where He alone sustains us.

Downsizing to Survive

You may be reading this chapter while experiencing the worst of times. Perhaps you have lost your home, your employment or even your career. Financially, your debit card is used up while your credit cards are maxed out. Putting food on the table means selling your plasma or finding something that a pawnshop will accept. Tears come far faster than sleep. World events have no meaning to you because your personal world has more crisis than you can possibly manage.

We need not be ashamed when we must downsize to survive. The ancient Egyptian people sold all they had to Pharaoh to endure the seven lean years foretold by God through Joseph (Genesis 47:15-20). Jacob, upon being presented to that same Ruler, remarked that "few and unpleasant have been the years of my life" (Genesis 47:9, NASB). That is hard fact, not whining or complaining. Like many families, my dad's dad lost his home and all he had during the Great Depression. Like Jacob, he moved to a new location to find work and to start over again. *From time to time, God moves us by undoing us.*

Jesus promised that "In this world you will have trouble" (John 16:33, NIV). Echoing that theme, Paul reminded Timothy that "in the last days, difficult times will come" (2 Timothy 3:1, NASB). Our Father takes the great and small alike through the boiling pot of hardship. Do you need an example? Look no further than King David, the very one whom God called "a man after His own heart" (1 Samuel 13:14, KJV). Life should have been easy after he killed Goliath. After all, he was a hero and heroes live happily ever after, don't they? "Only in Hollywood," as they say on the street. This same loyal, godly hero was pursued by King Saul, whose fortunes he had saved, lived in caves before he lived in a palace, endured attempts on his life, engaged in warfare during most of his reign, knew disdain from those he wisely led, was saddened by a dysfunctional family and a spouse who treated him with contempt, experienced rejection and an attempted coup by his favorite son, and lived with a host of issues that would leave any of us reeling. Do you feel as though your efforts lead only to heartache? Even Jesus, through the words of Isaiah, stated that "I have toiled in vain, I have spent my strength for nothing and vanity" (Isaiah 49:4, NASB). Being Christian offers no insulation in this life against the certainty of adversity.

Note well, however, Our Father's compassion for our plight:

> "You have taken account of my wanderings;
> Put my tears in Your bottle.
> Are they not in Your book?" Psalm 56:8, NASB

Think of it! Every tear we shed touches Our Father's heart so much that He records them in a special book! That is how close our heartache is to His heart. Such a One as He will never ignore us in our hours of crisis.

Marti works with kids at her school who have their little worlds torn apart by the reversals of fortune experienced by all kinds of families. When they sadly come to her to say they are moving, she first feigns indignation: "You can't leave, we love you too much!" she says with humor. Then reassuring them that they will be missed and that all are sad to see them leave, Marti asks, "Tell me about your new, exciting adventure!" Get the connection here, please. *Like the counselor for those struggling children, Our Father implores us to reframe our fears into possibilities. His plan for us is filled with opportunity and potential.*

Holding on and grieving is an important tribute to the importance of loss. It is, after all, why we have funerals and cemeteries. As I have told many clients, the hardest walk we will probably ever make is away from the graveside after we have lost a spouse, a child or a close loved one or friend. Do not minimize your loss nor dwell on it to the exclusion of God's grace in your crisis moment. Loss is to life what a tent is to a dwelling place: it is only temporary, not our permanent abode.

Along adversity's road, we relearn the values of frugality, camaraderie, gratitude, hospitality, patience, perseverance, dependence and faithfulness so that we may become better subjects for Our Father's kingdom now and in the eternal life to come. Those same virtues serve us well in our every day routines. How many of us are ever so much better off for having been raised with that venerable New England ethic of "use it up, wear it out, make it do or do without?" Or perhaps you learned as I did that "family always sticks together?" Here is another: "one hand for yourself and the other for the ship." In business matters, I often recite to clients the old common law maxim that "he who would grow rich in a year will be hanged in six months. *When downsizing comes, we may be disappointed but we need not be afraid, for Our Father has equipped us with the tools and skills of survival.*

Use makes master. Our skills today are not entirely those of our ancestors. Try to picture Benjamin Franklin navigating a major city freeway system. Poor Richard's Almanac would never be the same! A "stitch in time saves nine" still works but leaving an hour early for a job interview works better still! *When you must greatly downsize, catalogue your skills and resources.* Writing down what you have and who you know starts the engine of a healthy adjustment to tough circumstances. Know what you know as well as what you do not know. Then apply those God-given gifts and talents to the project at hand, seeking help along the way. Check out what public and charitable services and goods may be available to you. Circulate. Talk with others constantly. Seek and you *will* find. Make the journey one of specific destinations from day to day, focusing on steps you may accomplish. Check them off as you do so because we all need to see progress. Laugh as much as you can. Fellowship as often as you can. And *avoid the temptation of dwelling exclusively upon your own troubles.*

Surprisingly often, the cure for our misery rests in looking beyond our own dark clouds. We have the choice of how we respond to the storm, both inwardly and outwardly. We may always choose to recognize that we are children of the King and the world is but a passing wind. Consider Jesus' words: "Are not two sparrows sold for a cent? And yet not one of them will fall to the ground apart from your Father. But the very hairs of your head are all numbered. So do not fear; you are more valuable than many sparrows" (Matthew 10:29-31, NASB).

One of the great curses of serious illness or personal crisis is the desire of body, mind and soul to feed upon itself and the corresponding urgent need for repair and survival. We cannot avoid rendering self-aid when our life's blood is at stake. But the life blood of our spiritual psyche requires that we go beyond ourselves for the sake of others. *Faith takes its own particular root when we reach out to those who need an extra hand as they attempt to keep a strong grip on their own lifeboat.* Recall again the Two Greatest Commandments: to love the Lord our God with every fiber of our being and to love our neighbor as ourselves. By faith we praise God in adversity, trusting Him to value us more than sparrows. And by that same faith we rejoice when He calls us to pull on the oars of another's frail craft, trusting that He will keep us all afloat in his own miraculous way. In those times, like Jesus, we will be able to proclaim "'Yet what is due to me is in the LORD'S hand, and my reward is with my God'" (Isaiah 49:4, NIV).

Downsized from Birth

Smitty (not his real name) had the rough and weather-beaten look that comes early to some men who labor with their hands. Short and wizened, he had never finished elementary school but he had his PhD in the school of hard-knocks survival. Looking at it another way, you could say that Smitty was downsized from birth. He never had much in the way of possessions and, financially, he seemed to live on the edge of a personal Great Depression all the time. Career wise, he was just another hired hand, albeit a hard worker who was always there. The legal problem I helped him with at the beginning of my career was of the small change variety common to suburban attorneys, quickly solved and forgotten, buried amidst the boxes of closed manila folders that represent the struggles of good people trying to get by. It is curious how we sometimes serve an angel unawares.

That spring morning promised rain and probably thunderstorms. In the Dallas area, that type of weather draws only passing attention. Although we live on the fringes of tornado alley we do not dwell on it. Hail and strong winds are the more likely companions when the skies turn a particular shade of green-gray that causes outdoor activities to cease and mothers to be sure that the kids are somewhere safe. Smitty was, where else? at work that morning. The noise probably got his attention. When he looked out the door, he saw a Texas twister bearing down on the shop where he labored. Perhaps he was about to run for cover when a fellow worker lost his sanity and ran out into the path of the dark cloud churning its way directly towards them. Smitty never told me exactly what passed through his mind. I know only that he made a choice. Ignoring the sane, sensible path of personal safety, he ran after the becrazed co-worker, jumping on him, laying on him until the maddening wind had done its worst.

The national news picked up on the story and for a moment, Smitty was a hero. I saw him the next day at the hospital. Although covered with cuts, welts and bruises, he did not seem any different from the same rugged-and-calloused man who had walked into my office a year or two earlier. I suppose that is the point of it all. He really was *not* any different. *Smitty simply made the decision to not let his personal survival needs stand in the way of a chance to help someone else.* Reaching out beyond his own pressing circumstances, he made sure that the other guy, too, lived to fight another day. That sounds like a pretty good definition of a hero to me.

You may think of yourself as ill-favored from birth, having neither money nor fame, position nor prestige, education nor great skill. Were someone to check your family tree, he might find a rope hanging on the end of it. The places you have lived will never be famous for your having slept there. Society is more likely to ignore you than to name a school after you. Indeed, your downsizing is so much a part of you that it is hard for you to conceive of yourself as ever being anything other than ordinary. In fact, "ordinary" would seem like a promotion to you.

Perception is not always reality. Man looks on the outside but the Lord looks on the heart (1 Samuel 16:7). Our Father knows *your* heart. He knows the plans He has for you and the good works that He purposes you to do. Attitude alone disqualifies you. Birth does not. The David who slew Goliath was born to an inconsequential family. Education does not. John the Baptist grew up in the wilderness far from the great religious schools of the day, yet he was chosen to prepare the way for the Messiah. A poor career choice does not. Rahab was a harlot, yet she became a part of the lineage of Christ. Poverty does not. The widow who gave her mite was counted as mighty in the eyes of Jesus. Physical limitation does not. Bartimaeus was blind but showed great vision at the approach of The Light of the World while short Zaccheus caught Jesus' attention and made the most of his opportunity with Him. Obscurity does not. Moses was a nomadic shepherd with a criminal past. And recall that Peter was a fisherman and Ezekiel was an exile when God called each of them to greater things.

Name any and every defect of body, mind and spirit that causes you to lower your head and cry in secret. Jesus beckons you to cast every care, every failure, every shame, and every inadequacy upon Him without delay. He has promised to give you rest. The rest He gives you is from fear, fatalism and frustration. You are not doomed to a life of meaningless toil. The work you do matters, for with it you are building towards eternity. Staying the course takes far more courage than running away. By doing so, you too will assuredly be called to rescue those who flee into the storm.

Downsizing Because...

Just about any aspect of our life can be downsized for reasons as varied as the uniqueness of Our Father's design for each of us. Although upsetting to the status quo, we, like a truck on a slippery road, can gain better traction with a strong downshift.

Downsizing to Go into Training. Goals inspire us to reach for nobler heights. Without them, we may find ourselves languishing in a mediocrity that minimizes our abilities while drawing us into inertia and depression. Recall this basic lesson of physics: a body at rest tends to stay at rest while a body in motion tends to stay in motion. Take your dream and go into training with it!

As Paul explained, "Everyone who competes in the games goes into *strict* training" (1 Corinthians 9:25, NIV, emphasis added). "Strict" draws its meaning from the concept of discipline. As goes our training, so goes our goal. At the outset of World War I, the seemingly mild-mannered President Woodrow Wilson became single-minded and utterly ruthless in his determination to whip every man, woman and child in the United States into shape to win the war without regard to cost or hardship. Even cherished civil liberties were sacrificed to ensure that our enemies had not one whit of advantage.

Training downsizes us by sweating the frivolous and foolish practices and habits out of our system. Everything is measured by the yardstick of "will this help or hurt my advancement towards my goal?" If you have played competitive sports, you have some idea of the rigors and structure of schedule, diet, and exercise required to succeed. If you have gone on to college, mastered a musical instrument, become accomplished at a trade, or achieved a notable result in any enterprise, you have experienced a measure of the selfless obedience required to make a lasting contribution. But if you have fought Satan on your knees and in your heart month after month for your spouse, children, family, and friends and for those who are in peril, you have understood, as no one else can, the demands upon all your resources required for the attainment of victory in the Oldest War of all.

"Study to show thyself approved unto God," Paul told Timothy (2 Timothy 2:15, KJV). This is the backbone of all training that will endure into eternity. Neglect not your Bible, your prayer life nor your God-ordained priorities of worship, family, and service to others. When you downsize in such a fashion, you are upsizing your investment in Our Father's Heart.

Downsizing to Connect. In Acts, Chapter 2, Dr. Luke shows us not only the miraculous power and ministry begun at Pentecost but the sweetness of the relationship between those earliest believers. I stand in holy, silent awe before these words: "And all those who had believed were together and had all things in common" (Acts 2:44, NASB).

What rare and lovely fellowship we must surely be missing in this age of hollow-plenty! Surrounded by treasures of convenience and indulgence, we are so very, very poor! It is not that we desire to be hungry and impoverished or even that we are ungrateful for our blessings.

Rather, we crave that strong sense of belonging and community where we are valued without regard to our purse or person and where our identity merges with our sense of peace and purpose.

Sometimes we must choose to have less so that we can become more centered with others. Of what worth are our work and leisure if they distance us more and more from those with whom we would share our being? Would you care to be a workaholic who on his deathbed sees Jesus and hears Him saying, "I never meant for you to work so as to abandon all the people I placed in your life"? Or would you instead be known as one who seemed financially ordinary but lived close to many hearts? Look at it another way. *We show that we value our relationships more when we weed out encroachments on those opportunities to build bridges of friendship, fellowship and service.*

How we choose to connect tells us something of our progress in Christian maturity. Those early believers who stayed close to one another knew that their strength came, in part, from commonality. While it is true that we must be comfortable being alone if we are to be mentally healthy, we must also be comfortable with others in a variety of settings to be whole. Connecting only for a few isolated purposes now and again speaks of sadness and illness as surely as does flocking to every convention and crowd. Closeness presupposes a deepening of communication, a sharing of who we are and an acceptance of differences in others without judgment, albeit with discernment. Those skills come with practice. What better way to practice than by enjoying the company of both old and new acquaintances within and without the Body of Christ as Our Father gives us opportunity? Sometimes downsizing can, literally, be a picnic, especially on a sunny afternoon, surrounded by those with whom you will spend eternity.

Downsizing to Sharpen Our Focus. Like a pencil, we sometimes need to get rid of some unnecessary wood so that we can be sharp and focused. Where is it in our life that we just do not "get it" in some crucial area?

When Marti and I were training to become foster parents, I, like many men, had trouble with making a strong commitment to all the difficult and highly personal training. I was not sure if it was worth the effort and commitment. One day, I suddenly "got it" through an unexpected encounter. The instructor that cold February Saturday morning was struggling to enter the building with a baby, teaching gear and assorted kid paraphernalia. I offered to take the child. "Don't offer if you don't mean it," she cautioned me. I assured her I was serious and so for the balance of the day I took care of this child I had never seen before or would likely never see again. He turned out to be a so-called failure-to-thrive baby who was actually about six months old instead of my supposed six weeks old. Doing all I could for him that day, I realized that I could do nothing about his past or for his future. All I could do was to give him the best safe-harbor care I could for one day. Safe Harbor. That did it for me and I have been totally sold out ever since.

Consider what sharpening your focus might mean to you and others. Through it, Our Father might choose to reveal to you a personal safe harbor that allows you to accomplish a cherished goal while giving the gift of sanctuary to others.

Downsizing to Free Up Room. Clutter contaminates composure, at least for some of us. Now and again, I suspect, we all need to take stock of the stuff we have acquired. In the end analysis though, downsizing is less about the dramatic all-or-nothing life style adjustment and more about self-containment so that He may increase while we decrease. *We downsize to free up room for God.*

If your spiritual garage seems rather musty, its contents may need updating. What about a new small group or a fresh coat of service? If you have not visited the Christian bookstore in a while, treat yourself to some music and a new book. If your Bible looks a little too new, put it to work! Maybe you would enjoy exchanging Bibles with someone near and dear to you. If you are having trouble getting into church or fellowship, change your routine. Be creative and have some fun! Downsizing can mean a return to excitement and vitality brought on by a yearning for a clear spirit that hears Our Father's Heartbeat even when the whirlwind hurls stones at us.

Chapter 4

ACCEPTING NOT KNOWING

"...we have no power to face this vast army that is attacking us. We do not know what to do, but our eyes are upon you." 2 Chronicles 20:12, NIV

Nothing in the household is as powerful as the remote control. Forget the checkbook and the grocery list. He who possesses the remote control rules the world! I know it is something of an exaggeration but you quickly saw the point. We like to have things our way. We want to control our space as much as we can. When it comes to job satisfaction, the ability to exercise influence over our small slice of the pie may enable us to overlook crabby bosses, crowded conditions and below the norm benefits.

Perhaps it is because we consciously or subconsciously realize how illusive and rare "control" really is. As much or more as any prior generation, *we live with the absolute certainty of absolute uncertainty.* Our daily bread comes via a job that may be gone before sundown. Our vehicles break down, while we hang our heads down in amazement at how many things can bring us down in so short a period of time. Did anybody get the license number of that truck that hit us? We never saw it coming. And as one modern wag put it, we cannot prevent what we cannot predict.

Reminiscing about the old ways does not help. Besides, the old days were not perfect either, were they? How can we go back to pre-cybernetic days without losing the advantages and advances of technology, science and medicine, sociologic improvements, not to mention the personal friendships and experiences we would not otherwise have had? The problem is as old as Solomon. In fact, he grappled with it. Consider for a moment his hard-won piece of advice: "Do not say, 'Why were the old days better than these?' For it is not wise to ask such questions" (Ecclesiastes 7:10, NIV).

Why is not wise? And how can we live prosperously and calmly in the shadow of all turmoil?

Learning and Leaving the Past

Only a true history buff would remember "Tippecanoe and Tyler, too," much less care what it meant. For better or worse, there is nothing as stale as last year's headlines. Today's news duly reported and recorded in any newspaper (and they are scarce enough!), winds up in the trash or at the bottom of the birdcage in a matter of hours. The world does not merely march on; it races at nano-speed toward a future that blends with the present.

Old ways are quickly forgotten. While preparing to move to a new home in the early 1990s, my sons Cliff II and Jason were rummaging around in my old work equipment box. One of them dragged out a mechanical box with long vertical columns of the digits 0 through 9. It had a handle on it and there was a place on the box that showed the changing of the numbers. He looked at me and said "What's this?" He had never seen a comptometer before. Another son pulled out a smallish rectangular metal ruler-looking device with lots of numbers on it and a bar in the middle that moved back and forth. "What's this?" he asked. He had never seen a slide rule. Another pulled out a piece of cardboard with squiggly lines on it. "Dad, what does this thing do?" he queried. He had never seen an ink blotter before. On it went. A mere twenty years after I had acquired the skills to use those tools, they were as obsolete as the vinyl records and eight-track tapes stored away for old time's sake. Little did Cliff and Jason know that the computer model that they sometimes played with at Dad's office would, literally, end up in a State of Texas computer museum a mere dozen years later.

I am glad I learned the use of those old tools, but they were not the sum of all good things. Much the same can be said for experience. Without the lessons of history we would, of course, foolishly rewind and repeat all of humankind's old mistakes every generation. It is a painful way to be stupid, isn't it? So from time to time, we must reflect upon what we have learned from our past experiences. They are our best, personal teachers and may not be ignored without unpleasant consequences.

Like talented movie stars, our deeds of yesterday serve us far better in a supporting role. When we give them top billing on the marquee of today's main event, however, we invariably run into trouble. This can lead to mental health issues ranging from simple depression to profound delusional thinking that requires full-time psychiatric in-patient care. In troubled times, we may safely enjoy the pleasant addresses of yesteryear. But it cannot become our permanent residence.

Sometimes our shortcomings haunt us to the point of true distraction. It is then that we are most vulnerable to the "could-have, should-have, would-have" game. You know how it is played: "I lost my job last year. I could have had a better one but I didn't think our company would merge with that new outfit that let all of us go so I turned down the offer from that start-up group. I should have taken it and I would have if I had only known…" Dear me. How the old memories do make fools of all of us! There are never any winners in the could-have, should-have, would-have, game so why place your ante on the table? The game is rigged. Satan has stacked the deck and he will bluff you into despair if you let him deal the cards.

That is what Solomon was saying. Our Father, not our Adversary, holds the ways of the faithful in His Hands and Heart. The past need not concern you. Learn from it, cer-tainly, but leave it outside the inner circle of your life while moving ever forward to higher ground.

Free to Use Eternal Time

Time has a tendency to frustrate all of us, moving either too fast or too slow. In our early years, life takes *forever* to unfold. Yet as we grow older, the days pass by like a DVD at high speed, except when a crisis occurs. Then time seems to warp through twisted mutations, the likes of which we cannot explain. A loved one dies, a child suffers a serious illness or injury, financial woes befall us, relationships fall apart, our enemies bear down on us and the digital watch of our soul beats irregularly, causing sleepless nights and hazy days. In bewilderment we ask, "Does God understand such things? Is He really with us in the moments when we don't know why all of this is happening to us?"

Let us first consider the nature of time itself to Our Eternal Father. The Psalmist tells us, "Your throne was established long ago; you are from all eternity" (Psalm 93:2, NIV). As to Himself, why would God care about time? If He is God, "from everlasting to everlasting" (Psalm 90:2), why would time be important to Him? It is not for His benefit, certainly, because He cannot be limited by the combination of seconds, minutes and hours by which we count our days of travel. Nor is He limited by anything except what we imperfectly call His Divine Character. Rejoice at this revelation: *Our Father is always free to use the tool of time to assist the objects of His Love.*

He made the sun stand still for about a day when Joshua fought his epic battle against the Amorites (Joshua 10:5-14). When good king Hezekiah was near death, he prayed to the Lord for deliverance. As proof that His word of healing was real, God allowed Hezekiah to choose whether He should make the shadow on the sundial move forward or backward (2 Kings 20:8-11). Our Father can cause events to come together as rapidly or as slowly as He wills, for He is not limited by our concept of time and space.

Complete the follow-through. If He is Eternal God, then all the resources He created stand ready for His use. When Robinson Crusoe lay near death, he found in his sea-chest a Bible that a friend had packed away for him. Up to that point, Crusoe had been the model of self-reliance. And it was his undoing, for in relying on self, he ignored God's ways, choosing, instead, to live by his own compass. Until death beckoned. Opening that Bible in between fits of a strong illness, Crusoe stumbled across the words that changed his life: "Call upon Me in the day of trouble and I will deliver thee and you will honor Me" (Psalm 50:15, KJV).

Our Father has scattered similar promises liberally across the landscape of Scripture. Look no farther than a few of the Psalms for these assurances. "But you, O God, do see trouble and grief…you are the helper of the fatherless" (Psalm 10:14, NIV). "For you, LORD, have never forsaken those who seek you" (Psalm 9:10, NIV). "Behold, the eye of the LORD is on those who fear Him, On those who hope for His loving-kindness" (Psalm 33:18, NASB). "The angel of the LORD encamps around those who fear Him, And rescues them….But they who seek the LORD shall not be in want of any good thing" (Psalm 34:7, 10 NASB). In the moments where we stand most alone, He, alone, will always stand with us.

I write these words today as much to myself as to you, dear soul. In a few hours, I will go to a rural church and, joining with others, bury a close, long-time friend while I struggle with problems of work, family and finances, just like everyone else. At 54, I tell myself that I am not old enough to see friends die. Having worked heavily in the yard a few days ago, I easily ran four miles in 90 degree heat yesterday afternoon, just as I expect to do today. So I am not old yet, am I? But the years move ever more rapidly onward and I, like you, must move with them. One of my college professors explained that, unlike God's, our perception of time changes as we age. Consider it this way, he told us. When you are four years old, the distance from one Christmas to the next represents one-fourth of your life, but by the time you are 40, it represents one-fortieth of your life. We relate to time differently as we mature so time does indeed appear to speed up with age, even as our steps slow down.

As a child, I learned literature and poetry from my attorney-grandfather who mentored me in the sum and substance of life. When, like today, I am at a loss as to what to do, I take comfort from the words of British Poet Laureate Rudyard Kipling who said, "If you can fill the unforgiving minute with sixty seconds worth of distance run, Yours is the earth and everything that's in it…" ("If," Rudyard Kipling). That, too, is what Our Father calls us to do, to keep on keeping on, as our country friends might tell us. While He works through the countless evolutions and revolutions of our days and ways, we can do something constructive by using our allotment of time wisely. To do so, we must trust that He cares for us so completely that He will, in the long run, form all our disjointed jigsaw pieces into a completed work, worthy of His Signature, no matter how much or how little time it takes Him to do so. For today, that is enough, even though I do not know more.

Facing the Vast Army with Confidence

Let's return to the story of King Jehoshaphat. The writer of Second Chronicles tells us that a great multitude (2 Chronicles 20:2, NASB, KJV) was coming against the forces of Judah. You will recall that Judah was small, a mere two tribes, as opposed to the ten tribes of Israel. We may not know exactly how many soldiers the writer had in mind when he said "a great multitude" but we know the number was overwhelming. The King knew he faced an-nihilation. He did not have the manpower to stop such a horde of invaders. The opposing forces were already less than thirty miles away so there was no time to seek alli-ances and help from other nearby rulers.

King Jehoshaphat was on his own and afraid. Notice what he did not do. He did not take matters into his own hands. He placed those matters in God's hands, where they rightly belonged. *We find our strength to accept uncertainty by acknowledging Our Father's sovereignty and by acting in total reliance on Him.*

We must actively agree that Our Father is Lord of all. "But our God is in the heavens; He does whatever He pleases" (Psalm 115:3, NASB). If we stand in awe of Our Father, seeing Him in the every-day fabric of our life, we are but a hummingbird's breath away from His Heart. What is it that causes you to stop mid-stride in wonder of Our Lord? Is it a sunrise or sunset over some favored spot? Or perhaps it is the smile of your spouse, a child or a grand-child. Maybe the sea or the mountains or a wildflower or a shooting star raises you to proclaim "Hallelujah!"

I love of all of these things and yet I am mystified to silence by the orderliness of His Universe. My mind cannot grasp the higher mathematics, even though my dad was a math major who, with infinite patience, tried to instill in me the knowledge of equations. To this day, I cannot solve a first degree equation; much less do I dare tread the ground of polynomials, the quadratic and the higher mathematics of calculus and chaos theory. Some scholars speculate that matters as diverse as DNA and music have at their core a mathematics-based explanation. What wonder! What mysteries He has placed before us! Oh my soul, I am but the smallest of particles in His relationship-creation yet it has pleased Our Father to allow me, to allow all of us, to contemplate it. Our Father has "set *eternity* in the hearts of men" (Ecclesiastes 3:11, NIV, emphasis added)! Well did the Psalmist David speak when he said "O LORD, our Lord, how majestic is your name in all the earth!" (Psalm 8:9, NIV).

If you have lost touch with the child within you, go a place where you have seen God most clearly in the past. Or recall a time in which you stood as one dumbfounded by a riddle of creation. I remember clearly one such instance. It was in church one pleasant, sunny day where I sat with my dear grandmother. At the age of about eight years old, the sermon meant little to me, but Our Father taught me that morning in a different way. In the pew in front of us, a baby, perhaps six months old, was playing with a set of plastic rings-on-a-chain that most of us have seen many times. That morning, I *saw, really saw*, the beauty of creation in a child as I sat, unable to move, watching this baby explore his small world. I would later learn that I am "fearfully and wonderfully made" (Psalm 139:14, NIV). But I already knew, first-hand, what David meant. Maybe he had been watching a child play with a toy, too, when he wrote those words.

If you are moved to tears by the work of His hands, accept the blessing. The saddest of all creatures may well be those who are too dry-eyed to be passionate about anything other than a football score or a bargain at the shopping mall. *How little we know about anything!* If it moves us sometimes to tears of frustration, how much more so may we rejoice when our not knowing draws us closer to Our Father?

Sometimes not knowing takes on a potentially catastrophic dimension. As a young child, I recall those familiar faces in our Dallas neighborhood beating back a grass fire of some hundreds of acres with only tow sacks, brooms and, finally, garden water hoses, all the while not knowing whether their houses would remain intact. Many of you have seen tornadoes up close, as have I, along with floods of water, catastrophic illness, great financial setbacks and other severe misfortunes. What are we to do at such times?

What we may not do is choose God by default. Looking back on King Jehoshaphat, note carefully that he *immediately* sought God's help, without once taking the pulse of those around him. Our Father honors the decisive move to His side as we forsake all others. "The eyes of the LORD range throughout the earth to strengthen those whose hearts are fully committed to him" (2 Chronicles 16:9, NIV).

Having fasted and prayed with all the people, the King received his answer. But *he still had to finish in the Lord what he had begun.* Sometimes, His instructions seem, well, a little unbelievable. What military general would send musicians to the front of an under-manned army to loudly sing praises to our God as they approached the enemy? Note the conclusion of the story. The Lord set ambushes and totally confused the Ammonites, Moabites and Seirites who attacked and destroyed each other. The lesson? Turn the tables on confusion by allowing the improbable ways of Our Father to take their course.

Risking repetition, I share with you the timeless truth that what God has done before, He will do again. Have you, like the Psalmist, stretched out untiring hands at night as you sought to be comforted? Have you been too troubled to speak? The Psalmist Asaph provides the answer: "Then I thought, 'To this I will appeal: the years of the right hand of the Most High.' I will remember the deeds of the LORD; yes, I will remember your miracles of long ago. I will meditate on all your works and consider all your mighty deeds" (Psalm 77: 10-12, NIV).

When you do not know what to do, remember Who does know. Seek Him quickly. Stand in awe of His works and ways and do not be upset by your own limitations. Accept, even embrace, the not knowing. Expect His perfect-unexpected, acting in confidence when He moves. Oh, and remember to smile. Our Father and all those with Him love watching you succeed.

Chapter 5

THE WONDER OF ULTIMATE REALITY

"In the beginning God...." Genesis 1:1, NASB

"O LORD my God, you are very great; you are clothed with splendor and majesty. He wraps himself in light as with a garment;" Psalm 104:1-2, NIV

"This is how God showed his love among us: He sent his one and only Son into the world that we might live through him." 1 John 4:9, NIV

Nothing can prepare you for your first trip to the Caribbean. When our family went there over Christmas recently, we kidded everyone that we were having a "white-sand" Christmas. Nor can words describe the mixed shades of blue and green found in the sea, on land and in the sky. One might as well attempt to reduce the works of Mozart, Brahms and Bach to a few stanzas of melody or a State Dinner to hors d'oeuvres. We can soak up the sun but we cannot convey the glories of its rising and setting.

Human speech fails far more miserably in its attempts to describe and define God. That is our starting point for this time we share together. We are as the merest of children when it comes to touching the Ultimate Reality that is Our Father. Imagine for a moment a barnacle trying to describe a whale and you sense something of the dilemma, indeed, the frustration, of putting down in hard words the essence of the Godhead. With the best will in the world, we will fall far short of the mark.

And that is why God has left us a record of Himself, in which He reveals what He considers needful for us sojourners of this life under the sun. His words in the Bible stand faithfully as a beacon for all who would know the safe channel to His harbor. From them, we may come to some sense of what we loosely call His Attributes or Character. Our personal experience in walking with Him will demonstrate His faithfulness, His mercy, His compassion far more than any human interpretation. Just like those Caribbean nights, His cool breezes will wash over and refresh us all of our days if we will but yield to His gentle Hand.

No Other God Will Do

Do you ever wake up on a non-work day morning, reach into the closet and grab the first clothing you can reach? I enjoy days like that, don't you, those days where any old clothes will do? How we clothe ourselves helps define who we are. Perhaps you remember learning these lines from William Shakespeare's *Hamlet*: "Costly thy habit as thy purse can buy, but not expressed in fancy; rich, not gaudy: For the apparel oft proclaims the man." So my courtroom suit will be as out of place with my lawnmower as my briefcase is with my soiled gardening jeans.

How we clothe God in our thoughts says a very great deal about our relationship with Him. Do we see Him as far-off or as the real, personal, I AM who cares about every aspect of who we are and what we are doing? Do we view God as a laissez-faire Creator who, having set the wheels of planet Earth and its inhabitants in motion, has gone on to better things? Do we wrap Him in the pedestrian garment of polytheism, believing Him to be just one of many possible gods and but one of many cattle-paths to a possible heaven? Let me ask it this way: deep inside, will any old god do for you?

Go back in time with me to the point where there was no time. God was there. Define to your satisfaction the beginning of all things and you will find The Creator before you find the created. We learned in science class that no effect is greater than its cause. Follow the principle, metaphysically, for a moment. What is a void? It is the absence of matter. But is not even a void *something*? And how did that void get here in the first place? Is the everyday world around us all there is? Or could it just be that we truly know only in part as Paul says in 1 Corinthians 13:9?

Our concept of ultimate reality breaks down without a beginning. And so we are led by a seemingly genetic-spiritual compass-logic to the words, "In the beginning God." Out of the unfathomable chaos of the cosmos we find not just matter but He Who created and made sense of all matter and of all that matters to each of us. The stars did not light themselves. They were lit. And if they were lit, does it not appear that the Intelligence that lit all the fires of creation has never ceased His work with that which He started? Would One such as Him abandon what He began? To do so would mean that God abandons Himself. By definition, only God can be, *must* be true to Himself, otherwise He is false and His laws both scientific and spiritual are flawed such that they cannot be relied upon.

"False in one thing, false in all things" goes the old expression, derived from Latin. Our God is not a liar, despite the disbelief of a world that accepts evolution without an Evolutor. "What if some did not have faith? Will their lack of faith nullify God's faithfulness? Not at all! Let God be true, and every man a liar. As it is written: 'So that you may be proved right when You speak and prevail when You judge'" (Romans 3:3-4, NIV). Therefore, isn't it true that our God must be perfect?

Even in our own gnat-like intellect, we can instantly see that the perfection of the Perfect One far exceeds our ability to comprehend Him, without assistance from Him. When we speak of "perfect days" do they not inherently incorporate reference to His perfect creation of sun-filled mornings and starry nights, of sunrises and sunsets, of heat and cold, storm and calm? Does He want us to understand Him in a significant way or merely to go rushing along like the maddening wind of a Santa Ana, blowing this way and that without any reference to its Author or its Author's purpose and plan? These things cannot be if He be God.

If He desires that we know Him, could this perfect God abandon His creation? If we accept that we are made in His image, we will understand how this cannot be so. Take your favorite labor or pastime. When you achieve success in or with it, do you immediately discard or discredit it? Of course not! The bowling trophy, the thank-you note or award, the softball team jersey, the favorite rosebush or flowerbed receive special treatment for they are the stuff of worthwhile achievements and pleasant memories. Dear Soul, are we not much more valuable to Our Father than the souvenirs of our better days?

If Our Father has not abandoned His creation, neither has He abandoned any one of us. We are worth much more than the many sparrows for which He also provides (Matthew 10:31). Yes, He knows our imperfections, our spiritual high crimes and misdemeanors. But they do not keep Him from our side because the work of His equally Perfect Son, Christ Our Lord, allows peace between the imperfect and the Perfect (Romans 5:1).

Our Father, alone, is Ultimate Reality. No other god can do what He has done and continues to do actively in His creation: bringing all humankind into harmony with Him and with each other through Christ. No other Way will work, otherwise Our Father would not have allowed His Son to die on the Cross. Think of it in human terms for a moment. Would you allow any beloved family member or friend to die if you could avoid it? Neither would Our Father.

We are neither naive nor simplistic. The world's problems confront us at the drop of a website. Like Paul, we are "perplexed, but not in despair; persecuted, but not abandoned; struck down, but not destroyed" (2 Corinthians 4:8-9, NIV). And the truth of it becomes all the more apparent as we cultivate right-thinking about Our God and Our Father.

Holy Ground: Considering the Eternal Presence of God

Here we turn onto the gravel path, the road that is less frequented. Many will know *of* God. Few will *seek to know* God. "Immortal, Invisible, God Only Wise; In Light Inaccessible, hid from our eyes; Most Glorious, Most Splendid, The Ancient of Days: Almighty, Victorious, Thy Great Name we praise!" exalts the old hymn. Our Burning Bush bids us draw near. Taking off our shoes, we stand on holy ground as we confront the magnificent folly the world refuses to accept: that Our Father would engage us in divine fellowship.

We cannot imagine Him, re-create Him in art or describe Him in words. All attempts to do so border on the sacrilegious, for Almighty God defies all that is mortal and tangible. Yet it pleases Him to reveal His Eternal Presence to us in ways that cannot be numbered. Because He is without boundaries except those which He creates, we may consider Our Righteous Father through what He has shown us of Himself through Holy Writ and Divine Creation. We will touch but the smallest part of His Lofty Being. But even that merest of particles of The Godhead will sustain us until that glorious time when faith becomes sight.

Do not deny us Thyself, Oh Father Who Art in Heaven! Like Thy servant David, we would ask but one thing of Thee: that we may dwell in your house all our days, gazing upon Your beauty (Psalm 27:4). May it please Thee now to dim the shadow of our soulful ignorance by granting us a glimpse of those wonders that the happy inhabitants of Thy Kingdom which has no end, enjoy with unending praise to Thee.

Dear Soul, what follows is but a poor beginning to what may loosely, reverently be ascribed as attributes of God. They are without end and will occupy your meditations all your days. You will see them in different ways, in different shades and in different times as His Holy Spirit directs. The point is this: we have misplaced our desire for a hunger for God, filling it instead with the junk fast-food of worldly interests. By thinking about the Revealed God, we can combat the malnutrition of spirit that gives rise to every evil desire.

He Is Present In His Eternal Nature. Like Ezekiel who saw the "appearance of the likeness of the glory of the LORD" (Ezekiel 1:28, NASB), we must resort to simile and metaphor to consider the Eternal Being of God. He is *un*like any other, hence the inadequacy of human interpretation. In describing what he saw, Ezekiel uses the words translated as "like" or "likeness," "resembling" or "resembled" and "appearance" some 25 times in the first chapter of the book that bears his name. How else could he convey any sense of the indescribable scene set forth before him?

We also have difficulty in conveying the wonder of the Eternal. Have you ever tried to describe the emotions that filled you when you held your first child for the first time? Or what about the marriage to the great love of your life, can you talk about it in intelligible words or are you, like me, reduced to meaningless gibberish? Well did the poet speak when he asked "For the depths, of what use is language?" ("Silence," Edgar Lee Masters).

As we consider the forever-ness of God, we must abandon all linear concepts for He can be defined in neither analog nor digital dimensions. Of Him, Moses said, "Before the mountains were born or You gave birth to the earth and the world, Even from everlasting to everlasting, You are God" (Psalm 90:2, NASB). Speaking to John the Apostle, God spoke this of Himself: "I am the Alpha and the Omega… who is and who was and who is to come, the Almighty" (Revelation 1:8, NASB).

Wonder of Wonders! The God who created all things is also the God of Kindergarten letters, who teaches us our A-B-Cs! He is both beginning and end but has neither end nor beginning!

He Is Present In His Constancy. Perhaps you were required in school to memorize these oft-quoted lines from Shakespeare: "This above all: to thine own self be true. And it must follow as the night, the day. Thou canst not then be false to any man." It's a nice thought, but imperfect man, with the best of intentions, cannot be perfectly true, especially if he is not first true to Our Father. Only God can be true to Himself and, hence, to His creation.

Oh, but how vast and wondrous is His faithfulness! All that is heaven and earth rests on His constant, unchanging natural and spiritual laws! If He were not faithful then neither would be the laws of gravity, light nor sound. If He were not true, then in what and on whom could we believe? Peter understood it. When Jesus was deserted by so many and asked if His disciples would also leave Him, Peter answered, "Lord, to whom shall we go? You have the words of eternal life" (John 6:68, NIV).

"Thou changest not. Thy compassions, they fail not. As Thou hast been, Thou forever shalt be." So goes one of the great songs of all hymnody, "Great is Thy Faithfulness." Can we conceive but the smallest part of what those words convey? If God were not perfectly constant, one could argue that He was in some way imperfect. If He were imperfect, would that not leave room for the possibility of another god to compete with Him? And might not that god have different laws that would behave in opposition to those of Our Father? Yet all creation, all that we call "nature," works in perfect harmony. We need never ask whether the sun will rise or the tides return. Season follows season. We breathe an unchanging atmosphere, altered only by man's excesses. The animal kingdom follows its own laws of birth, death and survival. While man may rearrange the pieces of creation, he does not bring matter into existence.

Nor need we ask whether His love will ever fail. Because He is constant in all things, all of His attributes are equally present in all things at all times. "Weeping may last for the night", the psalmist wrote, "But a shout of joy comes in the morning" (Psalm 30:5, NASB). Declare, then, your eternal triumph in Him who never knows defeat! You are a child of the King and you share in the victory if, indeed, you have accepted all that He Is through Christ Our Lord.

He Is Present In His Eternal Compassion For Humankind. Children have an interesting way of explaining life. A very young student walked up to my counselor-wife Marti with a piece of an animal cracker in each hand one afternoon. "A rhino and a cow," he explained. "They both taste the same. Life is really messed up!"

While we may chuckle at the animal cracker logic, we do so recognizing the merit of the statement. Life *is* messed up. It is OK to say so. God is not at all unhappy with us when we state the obvious. Nor is He angry with us when we ask the hard questions of life. Ask any hard question you choose, this very moment. In fact, I will start off with not one but two of them. Why is there so much suffering in this world even among the good and decent folks? Why isn't God doing more for them? I am not ashamed of my hard questions and you should not be either. While we explore mine, you may be surprised at how your own questions come into perspective.

Our Father created a perfect world and placed there, in a particular garden, a certain Adam and his wife, Eve. Yes, you know all about it. But *do* you, really? Their story is our story, the story of choice and consequence. Bad choices equal bad results. Usually we know when we are behaving foolishly. All humankind makes an endless litany of bad choices over a lifetime. Most of the time, we learn from them and go on. But all choices have a ripple effect. Compounded thousands of times over billions of people, we dwell in a tidal wave of consequence that threatens to annihilate our world, not merely our peace of mind.

Would you take the high road of optimism for a moment, agreeing with me that most people try to do the right thing most of the time? It is still not enough. As we see all the time in the courtroom, reasonable minds can differ on what is and is not legally acceptable behavior. Recall, now, God's perfection. His moral standard is absolute perfection. No wrong choices. Ever. And we can never measure up on our own.

God has answered my questions already. First, there is suffering because of bad choices. And I must allow for God's sovereignty in choosing me to suffer for His sake, at certain times and in certain circumstances. If I serve a King, I must be ready to take a few blows now and then. If

Job could endure the loss of all he had and still proclaim, "The LORD gave and the LORD has taken away. Blessed be the name of the LORD." (Job 2:21, NASB), so must I also be ready to do the same.

And God has done and is doing more than I could ever imagine, for He has granted me the perfect compassion of Christ. Paul expressed it this way to the troubled Corinthian church: "Blessed be the God and Father of our Lord Jesus Christ, the Father of mercies and God of all comfort, who comforts us in all our affliction so that we may be able to comfort those who are in any affliction with the comfort with which we ourselves are comforted by God. For just as the sufferings of Christ are ours in abundance, so also our comfort is abundant through Christ" (2 Corinthians 1:3-5, NASB).

He comforts us. We comfort others. He forgives. We forgive. He provides daily bread. We perform the good works He has prepared for us from the foundations of the earth (Ephesians 2:10). God uses human hands in many unforeseen ways. Please share this exercise with me. Consider one decent act someone has done for you in the past week. Next consider one good deed you have done for someone else. Are you with me? Now thank Our Father for both the act received and the opportunity for service to another. They are one and the same. Though they are seemingly small crumbs, they are still gifts from Our Father.

When our animal crackers are broken and tasteless, Our Father always comforts us through His own perfect means. Sometimes, he uses the hands of friends and strangers alike to bring relief when and where we least expect it. If it has not yet happened to you, know with certainty that you will be given the opportunity some day to be Our Father's anonymous angel-unawares.

He is Present in His Eternal Wisdom and Good Counsel. We will know no greater friend than Jesus, no wiser counsel than that which we have in His Holy Word, which His Holy Spirit helps us to understand.

One of the algebraic peculiarities rests in the fact that a quadratic equation has two solutions, both equally correct. God, also, has more than one solution to our problems but all of them both begin and end with Him. "The fear of the LORD is the beginning of wisdom," wrote Solomon (Proverbs 9:10, NIV). And Solomon concluded his great treatise on the futility of life without God by proclaiming, "Now all has been heard; here is the conclusion of the matter: Fear God and keep His commandments, for this is the whole duty of man" (Ecclesiastes 12:13, NIV).

It is Our Father, alone, who keeps us from trouble by the Voice of His wise counsel. At the end of his life, when Moses gave his final public instructions on God's Law to those children of Israel who had survived the forty years of desert wanderings, he charged them to "Take to heart all the words I have solemnly declared to you this day, so that you may command your children to obey carefully all the words of this law. They are not just idle words for you—they are your life" (Deuteronomy 32:46-47, NIV). God's Wisdom promises, "For whoever finds Me finds life and receives favor from the Lord" (Proverbs 8:35, NIV).

Contrast the Wisdom of God with the advice of the world. Take your fill of media entertainment and website nonsense. What do they offer? Mostly, they offer mere carnal indulgence and sugar-coated poison. Yes, it *is* a harsh assessment. Death is not kind. Eternal death is crueler than anything we can imagine. We choose our destiny by the advice we heed. Wise counsel leads to life. Fools follow after their own kind, indulging themselves in all forms of human mischief. You may only choose one road, one solution. Choose the gravel path that leads to His Door.

He Is Present in His Eternal Justice, Mercy and Grace. When clients come to me with a case, I tell them that at the end of the day, all they will receive from a judge or jury is a decision. They may or may not receive "justice" in some measure. The reason should be obvious: imperfect man is capable only of an imperfect righteousness. I conclude by telling prospective litigants that if they seek something other than a decision at the conclusion of a lawsuit, they should take their money and go enjoy a good vacation instead.

Do we need any more headlines to beat us blind with the message that man is cruel, being at best unequal in his regard for his fellow humans? God in His Wisdom is wise, alone. It thus follows that Our Father, alone, can render perfect justice. He *Is* perfect justice, even as sand, by its nature, is sandy and water by its nature cannot help but be wet. In law school we learned that jurisdiction is the authority of a court to pronounce judgment. A Court must have jurisdiction, or authority, over both the person and the subject matter of the controversy. A court may be given authority to hear divorce cases and not criminal cases in one state or area but down the road a few miles, another court may be able to hear both divorce and criminal cases. Do not expect it to make sense. It does not and never will. Nor will human decrees ever achieve perfect consistency.

Our Father uses the things of this world to show us His constancy by the inconsistency of human institutions and inventions.

A dear mentor and friend tells the story of a particular law school professor many years ago who was well known for giving the same examination at the conclusion of the course, year after year. One student confronted him with it, asking why he didn't change the exam because everyone always knew what he was looking for. His reply may surprise you: "I don't change the exam; I change the answers!" Our God is not like that. His answers are always the same, in every generation.

What God calls "sin" is justly sin. What He calls good must forever be good. It is we who must accept His ways and conform ourselves to His standards, just as any attorney, any litigant, must conform to the thousands of rules and particles of law that form a part of any case. But catch another fundamental difference. Whereas "ignorance of the law is no excuse," God's grace and mercy supply hope and a way out of the devastating penalties for disobedience to His law.

Enter the role of redemption. Justice, like a tiger's appetite, must be satisfied. Hence, we are commanded by Christ to settle with our adversary while we are on our way to court lest we receive the full punishment for our offenses (Matthew 5:25-26). God's Judgment says "I and My Holy Justice have been greatly offended but Christ has paid the death penalty once for all. Therefore my Justice has been satisfied and all who would come to me may do so freely." Mercy may only begin where Holy Justice has been paid its due. By grace, God bestows His Good Favor upon all who seek Him according to His Way and ways.

I am staring, right now, at a bookshelf full of volumes of law. They contain many thousands of pages of man's best efforts to govern himself wisely and well. In the hundreds of rules I follow on behalf of my clients every day, I do not once see the words "mercy" or "grace." Under human interpretation, "law" and "mercy/grace" remain in perpetual opposition. Of all the daily miracles I encounter, none so touches me as the immutable fact that a Loving God provides a way through the maelstrom of soulless law to His all-merciful, gracious, loving and gentle heart where He is ever present for all who are in need of sanctuary. He is even available to lawyers.

Avoiding the Pig-ishness of Life

Being in the business of controversy, I am no stranger to down-and-dirty hostility. Some attorneys have made their reputation and their fortunes on a practice of scorched-earth litigation tactics. When I encounter those sadly aggressive warriors who have not learned that a good case speaks better on its merits than on its anger and angst, I have to remind myself of an old lesson: beware of a mud slinging contest with a pig. You will only get dirty and, besides, the pig loves it.

Our Father earnestly seeks our company but we must first choose to leave the pigpen. When the prodigal son came to his senses, he quickly decided that life with the pigs could not compare with being even the simplest of servants in his father's house (Luke 15: 15-20). Nothing else was required. Nor need you spend days on the road to return to Our Father's home.

Let the pigs have their own way. For you, no other God will do. He is eternally present in ways that will capture your heart and captivate your spirit no matter what mud may come your way.

Chapter 6

FROM RESIGNATION TO RESILIENCY

...there was given me a thorn in my flesh...Three times I pleaded with the Lord to take it away from me. But he said to me, "My grace is sufficient for you, for my power is made perfect in weakness." 2 Corinthians 12:7-9, NIV

Neither Marti nor I typically lose sleep over what we hear from the media, so I was surprised one Saturday morning to find that my better half had been up much of the night because she was disturbed over the presentation of a radio evangelist. "He was just so negative," Marti explained. "He talked as though we are all totally fouled up in everything we do. All we can do is to ask forgiveness and maybe, if we are lucky, God will hear us. Whatever happened to *grace*?"

You can see one of the reasons why I married Marti. She has a habit of getting to the heart of things with great compassion and little fuss. We spent our errand time that early Saturday morning discussing the conceptions and misconceptions of grace. And I suspect that each of us needs a restless night now and then to pull us back to the central truth of the overwhelming nature of Our Father's goodwill and loving-kindness towards us, through Christ, despite the thorns we bear.

To allow the gift of grace to become a conscious part of our everyday lives, we must carefully work past the negative junk that pervades the world's conceptions of God. *Grace allows us to travel from the pot-holed road of resignation about the journey of life to the grassy path of resiliency, so that we might live life joyfully and abundantly.* No matter how lost we might be, grace always directs our feet back to Our Father's heart.

The Battlefield of Words

Law school taught me the importance of words. Law practice continues to teach me the skill of defining my client's position with my words and with fighting the words chosen by my opponent. For instance, my adversary might say, "You abandoned the project so we do not owe your client any additional money." I would counter by saying, "Your client did not pay for the work that was performed so we had the right to walk away until your client paid us." You immediately see the importance of the argument, for if I am to prevail, I must effectively demonstrate that the other side committed the first wrong and that my client simply exercised a legal right to not throw good money after bad.

Satan, our Adversary, works far more skillfully. He says, "Certainly God loves you but He will love you more and you can get to heaven, or be more righteous when you get there, if you follow the rules." Which came first, the good deed or the good heart? Or, stated differently, do we work *to be* saved from our sins or do we work because we *are* saved from sins? One way leads only to rules. The other way leads to the Eternal Relationship. Which is which? Let's talk about it.

"Let's Make a Law"

From time to time, I am asked to make a presentation to school groups about what attorneys do. I have developed a short, fun talk called "let's make a law," which does just that. Allow me to share it with you.

Let's make a law. The law will be "no running in school." Sounds easy to understand, doesn't it? Not so fast, if you will pardon the pun. What does "no" mean? Does it mean you cannot run on the playground? Does it mean that you can run on the sidewalks on the weekend when school is not in session even if you can not run on those same sidewalks during a school day? What if some one is trying to harm you? Surely you can run away then. But what if the Principal tells you to stop, even though you are afraid; what then?

Do we really understand what "running" is? Maybe we need some expert help. Now, at this point, I take off my coat and tie and pull out my running shoes from my briefcase. Looking at the kids, I explain that I have lots of experience as a runner, that I have been trained and coached and I have even attended running classes. I have placed in lots of races and have run over 20 marathons (26.2 miles) including the Boston Marathon. That qualifies me as an "expert" because of my education, training and experience. I then proceed through different speeds of "running."

Is a fast walk, where one foot is always in contact with the ground, not "running" if it is done faster than a slow jog where both feet might be in the air for a millisecond? How fast do you have to go before running is not allowed? What if your legs are really short (I am only 5'5" tall)? If you have to take two steps to the one step someone very tall might take, is that impermissible running?

What does "in school" mean? Does it mean the sidewalks? What about the sidewalks across the street you might use to go to and from school? Depending on the layout of the school, the sidewalk across the street from the school offices might be closer to those offices than the sidewalk behind the school. Is it OK to run on the ball fields? What about the playground? Does it make any difference if we are playing on school property on the weekends when no one is there?

On and on we go. The kids usually get a kick out of the mental challenge of deciding a case whether I am or am not running in school based on these different issues. Sometimes, however, they get frustrated. They ask, "How can anyone ever know what the law *is*?"

Ah, now *there* is a good question. As my attorney-grandfather used to tell me, law is whatever a judge and jury say that it is. There is more to it than that, but you get the idea. We have tens of thousands of laws covering every conceivable kind of circumstance at every level of human interaction. That does not include the rules that attorneys work with to help keep cases moving forward. Just now, I counted the number of rules I have in my *Texas Rules of Civil Procedure* book. The number is 627, unless I miscounted. I do not plan on counting them again. That does not include rules of criminal procedure or the rules of evidence, nor the rules of appellate procedure that govern law practice in the state of Texas. Add to that the fact that each state has its own laws and rules, plus the United States government has *its* own laws and rules, plus you have separate regulations and rules for government agencies at the state and federal level. Oh, by the way, each local government has municipal ordinances of all kinds. And did I mention that local courts have separate rules of practice that tell you what to do in their specific courts?

Lions and tigers and bears, oh my! Will the untold millions of volumes of law in these good United States make us any better citizens, particularly if we do not even know what those laws are? Are we required to know *all* of the law because, as we have learned, ignorance of the law is no excuse? How hard must we try to do good in order to *be* good? *Law says, you must be perfect in all or you are guilty of being a lawbreaker.* Practically speaking, we know we just can't do it. Even the best attorneys only know a small fraction of the law. With the best of intentions and skill (and an adequate fee), they will help you attempt to understand the law and work through the problems of your case. But no one can guarantee the outcome. Or as one wise Christian judge told a group of us while I was in law school, "You can know heaven in its bliss and hell in its fury, but son, oh son, you can never know a jury."

Kids, remember the rules. And try not to run in school.

The Consolation of Grace; The Condemnation of Legalism
Will someone, *please,* give us some good news?

At the time of Christ, many hundreds of years of living under the Law of Moses had brought the people of Israel to exactly the same point. They knew the rules of our Holy God Almighty. They knew they could never live perfectly by them. Oh, some claimed to do so. But did it really get them anywhere? I remember running a race in a wooded, hilly park one cold spring day some years ago. About one-half mile from the finish line, a group of us near the front of the pack crested a hill which then dropped off precipitously, like some theme-park roller coaster. All we could do was run faster, *faster*, FASTER, as we tried not to fall. Our focus was not on the thrill of running or even the joy of the finish line. It was on watching our feet go forward without making a mistake. We made it through, but at the cost of strained muscles and legs that ached for days.

Religious law is like that. You try to keep up with its ever increasing demands. Go to church not once but three times a week. Don't forget the committee meeting, the food pantry drive, the birthday gift for the church secretary and the Sunday school party. Square your shoulders, tighten your belt and do your Christian duty. Read your Bible, give until it hurts, fast and pray, work but don't dare play. Smile, you are on Satan's billboard for you have unwittingly allowed him to choose the words and to convince you that he, not Our Father, has the right plan for you. "Don't step on the spiritual cracks or you will break your mother's back," he taunts us, like some bratty eight-year-old.

Our Adversary always wants to confuse us. He desperately attempts to persuade us to think only about what we are doing rather than the who and the why of our faith. The

Apostle Paul saw through the smoke-screen of legalism. Those who promoted it, he called "dogs" (Philippians 3:2, NASB). That's strong language, even today. But it is only the beginning of Paul's assault on do-it-yourself salvation. Speaking to those who knew the ways of Old Testament Law, Paul continues on. "Yet I could have confidence in myself if anyone could. If others have reason for confidence in their own efforts, I have even more! For I was circumcised when I was eight days old, having been born into a pure-blooded Jewish family that is a branch of the tribe of Benjamin. …What's more, I was a member of the Pharisees, who demanded the strictest obedience to the Jewish law. And zealous? Yes, in fact, I harshly persecuted the church. And I obeyed the Jewish law so carefully that I was never accused of any fault" (Philippians 3:4-6, NLT).

Wow, Paul! It sounds like you get the gold medal of religiosity! I bet you will have a marble mansion in heaven with platinum stars and titanium hinges on the front doors! I could *never* do what you have done! But, please dear saint, hear the rest of Paul's story. "I once thought all these things were so very important, but now I consider them worthless because of what Christ has done…I no longer count on my own goodness or my ability to obey God's law, but I trust Christ to save me. For God's way of making us right depends on faith" (Philippians 3:7, 9, NLT).

Please notice the turn of the "ship" from "me-ship" to relationship and kinship. All of our good works are wonderful if placed in the perspective of grace. Indeed, Our Father has prepared them for us (Ephesians 2:10). But we work because we love Him, not to earn something that we could never earn to begin with.

Look at it another way. Men, when we rush home from work, we do so to be with those we love, don't we? Marti is my best friend, my confidant and my greatest relationship treasure under the sun. I work because I love her and want to do right by her, not to earn the love she has already freely given to me. I do not do so out of any duty but because of love. In truth, Marti loved me before I loved her. Why, I will never know. She had her prayer team praying for the "us" after we met briefly one time, before I had a clue that she was even on the radar. When I understood Our Father's plan for me and *saw* Marti for the first time, I changed in ways I did not think were possible. As a result, I have enjoyed a sweetness of life I could never have foreseen. I do not deserve Marti. As one doctor friend reminded me shortly after we were married, "Cliff, you married *way* beyond yourself."

"We love, because He first loved us" (1 John 4:19, NASB). We do not deserve Christ. All of us are members of the Lost Tribe: lost sheep, lost coins and lost children (Luke 15:1-32). He searched for us when we were lost, when we didn't even know we were lost. Nor is our value to Our Father diminished by our lostness: it is dependent, instead, upon the price Our Father paid by sending Christ to satisfy the divine holy necessity of sinless perfection. It matters not that we are covered with the dirt and grime of our misdeeds, of our spiritual shortcomings and of our imperfections. Our Father only sees the Pearl of Great Price who has purchased us with the all-sufficient and supremely valuable heavenly currency of Jesus' blood. No other consideration need be paid. No other consideration *could* be paid without insult to Father, Son and Holy Spirit.

May I suggest that our vulnerability endears us to Our Father? That we would come to Him, despite the "fightings within, fears without" ("Just As I Am," Charlotte Elliot), demonstrates our faith in opposition to all the evidence that our Adversary heaps upon us. When confronted with a case that looks bleak, I tell clients that this is one time where they really do not want justice! We do not receive "justice" from Our Father, either. Instead, we receive mercy, for He bypasses the evidence against us and looks only to Our Christ who has offered Himself not just as Our Advocate but as Our Pardon, having already taken our punishment (Isaiah 53:5).

With the deepest yearnings of His Eternal Heart, Our Father implores us to come to Him, for come we must if we are to become members of the family. When we accept the gift, we, too, change in ways we cannot imagine so that the good works we do are solely works of the heart. By accepting Christ as our Bridegroom, we, too, marry far beyond ourselves in the heavenly realms.

Our Father calls it "grace." We may rightly call it the ultimate miracle. Grace is the bridge from the resignation that results from our frustrated, vain attempts to earn Our Father's gift to the joyful resiliency that allows us to rest in what He has provided.

Grace To *Us; Grace* Through *Us to Others*

If, as our parents used to tell us, an idle mind is the devils' workshop, many of us must think we are bound for the Promised Land, judging by all our doing-ness. If you are weary of activity and of acting a part, then exit stage left and accept the invitation to just be a child of Our Father.

"For this Good News—that God has prepared a place of rest—has been announced to us just as it was to them… For only we who believe can enter His place of rest" (Hebrews 4:2-3, NLT).

Grace equals rejuvenation, not apathy or inactivity or laziness. It is again Paul who catches the heavenly theme and exalts its chorus in a pantheon of praise: "Rejoice in the Lord always, I will say it again: Rejoice!" (Philippians 4:4, NIV). In whatever state he was in, Paul had learned to be content (Philippians 4:11, 13) because he could do all things through Christ who gave him strength. It is the same Christ Who Is of the Same Substance with Our Father, who has broken the Rules, those tablets of the old law, having met every condition of the law.

Our hope does not depend upon whether or not we run in school but whether we run to the Cross where we find salvation's grace, of Our Father, by Our Christ and for all people in which we may rest secure forever! Forgiveness in not a mere possibility; it is a cross-clad, blood-bound guarantee identical to that preached by Peter and believed upon by thousands on Pentecost morning (Acts 2:38)!

Dare we not smile at the thought that we are no different in our calling than those blessed and brave souls who stood with the early Church throughout its persecutions? Knowing this, we may peacefully live as partakers of grace, being certain that we are also intended to be buckets filled to overflowing with the Living Water of Christ for the sake of others. Paul's chains that encumbered him while awaiting trial before Caesar meant nothing. If death resulted he would be with Christ. If Paul lived, it would mean fruitful labor so that those around him would overflow with joy in Christ (Philippians 1:19-26).

Blessed propinquity! Like an elderly couple whose love has transcended human restraints so much that they even begin to look like one another, Paul, because of grace, looked more like Christ with each passing day. May it also be said of us upon our graduation to Heaven, that the delightful unmerited favor of Our Father so changed us over time that even the thorns we bore gave testimony to the Rose of Sharon whose Bloom we wore as the sweetest joy of our life.

Chapter 7

APPLYING PRACTICAL GRACE

"Therefore, as God's chosen people, holy and dearly loved, clothe yourselves with compassion, kindness, humility, gentleness and patience. Bear with each other and forgive whatever grievances you may have against one another. Forgive as the Lord forgave you. And over all these virtues put on love, which binds them all together in perfect unity." Colossians 3:12-14, NIV

We have, as it were, a journey *to* grace and a journey *through* grace. The former takes us to the Cross of Christ. The latter helps us carry the message of His Cross through our lives for the sake of others, a process that we may refer to as practical grace.

This is not about theology. It is about everyday living in a way that allows us to be who we are while growing our roots into the soil of grace so that we may produce the fruit of a life well-lived. My personal journey some years ago led me to the realization that my roots were but shallow, puny things that had failed to penetrate into the deeper soil where Living Water flowed in abundance. As a result, I was unhappy and unproductive in most aspects of my life. Knowing *about* grace was one thing. I knew I belonged to Christ. What I did not grasp was the *how-to* of grace.

Every legal case must have a theme. Failure to clearly identify the theme leaves the judge and jury immersed in a wealth of detail without a roadmap and the attorney without a focal point to which he may relate all the evidence. Our theme, then, for practical grace may be summed up in the three words I learned during those days of great spiritual crisis: *forgive, accept, understand*.

Each word is essential as is the order of the words. To forgive is to exercise towards others, in small measure, the mercy shown to us by Our Father. To accept others where they are, as they are, helping them in whatever way Our Father directs, involves the essence of love. We cannot accept or love someone else until we accept that we have been forgiven and have the capacity and responsibility to forgive others. Understanding others, when and even *if* it occurs, leads us deep into the mystery of individuality and of God's creative power in all that is humankind.

Forgive. Accept. Understand. Each word is a garment that clothes us with grace to live with those around us in empathy and peace.

The Drawbridge of Forgiveness

Marti works with kids and kid spats every day. On occasion she will use the analogy of a drawbridge. It works like this. All of us decide who we will let inside our castle and how far we will let them in. If we have been badly hurt and have not worked through it, we completely close our drawbridge to that person. When everything is again OK, we let the drawbridge down because we are once again on friendly terms with that person. Often, we let the drawbridge down a little at a time because we are unsure how the other person will respond and how we will, in turn, respond to them. After a hurtful confrontation, we are not the same and it takes time before we can lower the drawbridge to any meaningful degree.

The great point to remember is that any movement toward letting down the drawbridge is progress. Why? *Because forgiveness is both an act and a process.* We "forgive" in the sense of letting go of what hurts us, thereby allowing our arms the freedom to embrace those with whom we have been at odds. The challenge comes in living out that forgiveness in our day-to-day activities. We forgive but we do not forget. Something within us *enjoys* remembering how we were wronged. We want to strike back. And we do so, only to find that, in the end, an exchange of relationship nuclear weapons leaves us as contaminated as it does our opponent.

I find that I need a very great deal of forgiving. Traveling to the cross to accept the gift of salvation was comparatively easy in the abstract. Denying myself, taking up my cross daily and following Jesus each day is quite another matter. When I consider the story of the prodigal son, too often I realize that although I have returned to my Father's side, I am not ready to embrace the one who, like me, has slept with the pigs. My conscience arches its eyebrow at my foolish ways so often that I feel like a child who can never do right.

Self-forgiveness looms large on the list of things I do not do well. By temperament and by rearing, I am not a half-way person, being strongly energetic and passionate about life. If I do something, I try to do it to the best of my ability. But my ability falls far short of my desires. Ruefully, I remember the adage that "only the mediocre are always at their best." It does not help much. My spirit cries out, "What a fool I am!"

At the moment when I throw up my hands in utter self-disgust, I am reminded that even the Apostle Paul fought the "never getting it right" battle. "I do not understand what I do", he said. "For what I want to do I do not do but what I hate I do" (Romans 7:15, NIV). How can it be that as re-born children of Our Father, we still sometimes, many times, make such a mess of things? Paul answers the question this way: "So I find this law at work: When I want to do good, evil is right there with me. For in my inner being, I delight in God's law; but I see another law at work in the members of my body waging war against the law of my mind and making me a prisoner of the law of sin at work within my members" (Romans 7:21-23, NIV). We prodigals still live in spiritual tents. We have accepted Our Father's ticket home, purchased by the blood of Christ. But we are not home yet. And we will stumble many times before Jesus embraces us at the front door of our eternal home.

Paul, too, cried out "What a wretched man I am! Who will rescue me from this body of death?" Immediately, joyfully, he answers his own question: "Thanks be to God— through Jesus Christ our Lord!" (Romans 7:24-25, NIV). If we would know the perfect peace of self forgiveness, we need look no further than this: "Therefore, there is now no condemnation for those who are in Christ Jesus, because through Christ Jesus, the law of the Spirit of life set me free from the law of sin and death" (Romans 8:1-2, NIV). What we could not do for ourselves, "God did" (Romans 8:3, NASB).

God *did* forgive us and we must learn to live with it. We are *not* condemned. *We are all family.* My dear grandmother used to tell me, "*We always stick together.*" God love her, she was so close to the Kingdom of heaven! I need my brother, no matter what has passed between us for he is a part of me.

My drawbridge needs to be oiled and repaired. It has not come down often enough or far enough. In my spiritually rational moments, I realize that a sliver of Hell vanishes when I let down the drawbridge of forgiveness so that my brother may find a cordial, if not a perfect welcome into my life again. And, miracle of miracles, when I begin to open the drawbridge, the light that floods my darkened room comes straight from my Father's Heart.

The Cookie Dough of Acceptance

My mom's dad had a practical sense of humor. During my growing-up years, when I would have a dumb-kid moment or if I was a little too impressed with some accomplishment, he would chuckle and remind me that "God knows and I know that one of you is enough!" Then we would both laugh and go on. Many years later, I sometimes feel the Holy Spirit's presence speaking those same words to me with that same touch of humor.

Reality *is* a funny thing. I am not God's gift to humankind, so living with the certainty of my fallibility brings me to my knees quite often in laughter or tears, depending on the circumstances. I tell all my clients early on in a case that I want to hear their thoughts and ideas at every turn because *two heads are always better than one where one of the heads is mine.* That is not false modesty. It *is* hard fact. And I rather suspect that by now you are laughing along with me, because you, too, know, as Shakespeare said through the mouthpiece of Marc Antony, that "the fault, dear Brutus, lies not in our stars but in ourselves." Or as one wise man said, "we have met the enemy and he is us!"

Life has a habit of making fools of all of us on a regular basis, doesn't it? I dare not cast stones at the ineptitude of others because mine far outweighs them all. Jesus said it best: "And why worry about a speck in your friend's eye when you have a log in your own?...Stop judging others, and you will not be judged. For others will treat you as you treat them" (Matthew 7:3, 1-2, NLT).

Before I can deal with the stuff of others, I must first get my own house in order. And that will never totally happen in this life. At best, I am a ball of dough, half-worked and half-baked, awaiting the final transformation into a glorious, useful work fit for God's eternal table. Raw cookie dough can be agreeable in small quantities. But it does not compare with the finished product of a master baker. For some us, the dough still has far too many "nuts" in it. For others, the "sugar" is lacking or the "consistency" of the dough is not what it should be. We look at the mess and wonder how this will ever turn out to be worth a hoot.

Let me tell you a story. Some years ago, the kids had a bunch of their high school friends over one weekend evening. The gang of twenty or so had the usual mix of guys and gals. A few of the young gentlemen decided that chocolate chip cookies would be a hit. But there was only one problem: they knew little about the workings of a kitchen. Daughter Mary came and woke me up about midnight to advise me that things were getting, shall we say, a little lumpy. Arriving at the field of battle, I found that the reports were accurate. In short, we had a recipe for a product more suitable for industrial use as a building product (concrete blocks come to mind) than as a human food substance. I gathered the troops together and ushered the ladies away to a kinder, gentler place. Then, together, we went to work. A little flour here, an egg or two there, a dash of baking powder, a smidgen of salt (all done very scientifically, of course) and so on it went. I needn't tell you that the unbelieving females never expected anything good to come out of the oven. I seem to recall comments like "it takes a real man to make a disaster in the kitchen." Oh ye of little faith! An hour later, the kitchen was clean, the chocolate chip cookies had achieved immortality and the guys were smiling again.

Yes, He *can* raise a dead kitchen and a dead heart alike to life. He does so each time we hug the child, young or adult, who has erred. He does it through the myopic eyes of those who see just far enough ahead to grasp His hand tightly, accepting the grace that allows us to be OK with ourselves so that we may take the outstretched hand of the one next to us instead of slapping the unseen face in the dark moment.

My kitchen always needs cleaning. No matter how shining and spotless it appears on the outside, the dishwasher remains full of dirty dishes, hidden away where others cannot see. God knows, and I know that is reason enough for me to accept those around me in whatever condition they may be in at the moment.

On the Other Side of the Window: The Mystery of Understanding

From hard practice, we have all learned a precious smidgen about love. You have been in life's trenches where you have sat beside the cherished one in time of great crisis. You have comforted those who mourn. You have prayed for those whose loads are too much to bear. Your paychecks have supported family, government and ministry while your savings account has gathered dust. Life awards no medals for the daily heroism of devotion.

At my miserable best, I will know but little of the silent, thankless toil of those around me. And I will know even less of the greater mysteries of Our Father's Universe. But once in a while He favors us with a great insight, the understanding of which shapes our life, sharpens our focus, and enables us to share something valuable with others. Let me share the story of one such close encounter with Our Father's deep wisdom.

Perhaps you have been puzzled why Our Father occasionally allows the guilty to go free. I, too, struggled with this problem while I was in my early days of law school. One evening, I attended a dinner-fellowship sponsored by our Christian law students' association. The guest speaker was a local criminal court judge, much experienced in the ways of major, felony crimes and the individuals who perpetrated them. One student asked the judge the classic question of how he dealt with the problem of turning a criminal onto the streets on a mere technicality of the law, when the person was obviously guilty.

Listen to his answer: *"Never forget that every man stands condemned at the bar of his own conscience."* The judge went onto explain that the very thing for which the court is required to set him free, despite his obvious, over-whelming guilt, may be the very thing that brings him to his knees before God Almighty. We cannot judge the ways of God with His creatures.

That settled the issue with me forever and I have been at peace with it ever since. Only Our Father knows the heart of all. Only Our Father can reach each of us uniquely to bring us to the place of correction or comfort. Or as Marti reminds me when I become too judgmental on a matter, "You are not that person's Holy Spirit."

Well-spoken. Paul said it like this: "Now we see but a poor reflection, as in a mirror; then we shall see face to face. Now I know in part; then I shall know fully, even as I am fully known" (1 Corinthians 13:12, NIV). Have you ever looked outside through a heavily frosted window to a beautiful winter morning? You can see light and shapes to some degree, but you cannot discern what is truly on the other side of the window.

I cannot see beyond the window of my brother's soul. So I must content myself with forgiving and accepting him as much as ever I can. Over time, as our relationship grows, the Blessed Light may warm us sufficiently to allow a thaw to occur where I may see more deeply into his real self. That understanding will not come in a moment and when, if ever, it does occur, I will be more mystified than ever by the beauty of a life lived in an array of conflict and circumstances far beyond my power to comprehend.

Like Barabbas (Luke 23:18-25), I, too, have been released from prison and death because my Savior chose to accept my punishment. I, too, stand condemned at the bar of my own conscience. Because I do, I know something of my brother's angst. *Understanding is for those willing to take God's path wherever it leads them.* We do not know where He will guide us this day. But we know many others tread the way to higher ground. We may smile with the understanding that we share an uncommon thread that binds all together who call upon His name. And, blessed miracle! someday we will both know fully that which we dimly perceive on the other side of the window.

Chapter 8

AFTER THE FIRE, FLOWERS

While he was still speaking, a third messenger arrived with the news: "The fire of God has fallen from heaven and burned up your sheep and all the shepherds. I am the only one who escaped to tell you." Job 1:16, NLT

The message was not a good one. My mother, at the age of 44, was dying. The cancer had returned with a vengeance. Nothing was stopping it. Nothing, but God's own hand, would be able to stop it. Final exit. Checkmate. Game, set and match to death.

A sixteen-year-old boy does not think in terms of finality. That is for old people or for those in hospitals whose lights alone we see from busy streets where we ply our daily care. But it is not always so. Sometimes we must confront all that we fear as directly as a sudden fire that forms before us. Nothing may keep us from those moments.

"For the Depths, of What Use is Language?"

If I have learned any lessons about empathy and compassion, their beginnings must be traced to those many nights I stayed up with Mom, sharing the moments that have no name. Sometimes we talked about anything and everything. And sometimes we accepted the silence.

The American Poet Edgar Lee Masters expressed it this way in his poem "Silence":

"I have known the silence of the stars and of the sea;
And the silence of a city when it pauses.
And I have known the silence of a man and of a maid
And the silence for which music alone finds the word.

And I have known the silence of the sick as their eyes roam about the room
And I ask, 'For the depths, of what use is language?'"

The banality of ordinary conversation stands mute in the presence of eternal realities. Job's friends sat with him on the ground for seven days and seven nights before they said a word (Job 2:13). It was the one thing they did correctly. Certain disasters of the spirit render us mute. Wisdom bids us to honor the quiet moment, to "Be still, and know that I am God" (Psalm 46:10, NIV).

Events speak their own language to us. Loss knows its own vocabulary of the heart. Those who tread the byways of friendship serve well with an arm around the shoulder, a tightening of the grip in a handshake, a meal delivered, a yard mowed, a child comforted, a pet looked after.

When disaster renders us incapable of addressing the details of life, we derive comfort from the small graces others share with us. Turning them away does not ease our burden and makes them poorer in the bargain. If we would begin to heal, we must allow others to touch us in their own special ways. After Mom died, several friends of mine and a local teacher with whom we were close more or less forced me out the door to play tennis the afternoon before her funeral. In those moments, I was one of the boys again and I felt the first stirrings of Our Father's healing winds upon my spirit. Life would go on. I would finish growing up and move on to maturity. Hours would soon cease to feel like days. And the days would become routine again.

My counselor-wife Marti explains to those in grief that at first, you feel bad every minute. Then, over time, you have a few minutes where it does not hurt as badly. Eventually, you will have a good hour or two and, with process, you will at some point have an entire day that is rather good. Time may not fully heal our wounds if we do not allow ourselves to grieve fully. If we do, then those good days will become more frequent, the bad nights more bearable and we will pass through the storm, even as we always remember the fire which touched but did not overcome us.

Worry is Like a Rocking Chair

Humor is not absent, even in crisis. Mom kept a sewing box on the end table next to her rocking chair where we spent oh so many hours. One night she looked at me with that special twinkle in her blue eyes that made all of us smile and she said, "Cliff, if you do not remember anything else, I want you to remember this." And she pointed to a small wooden sign on that box which read, "Worry is like a rocking chair. Keeps you busy but never gets you anywhere." How we did laugh! And how many times I have laughed at the memory of it over the years.

If neurosis could be cured by a verse, surely that would do the trick! Can we not be amazed at the number of things that worry us to distraction that never happen or occur only to a more limited, bearable degree? What parent has not learned that threatening a child with dire consequences often produces the desired change in be-havior? Worriers of the world, unite! We have met the enemy and he is us! Like some Macbethian witch's brew, we stir the cauldron of concern to the point of madness. For what purpose? "Who of you by worrying can add a single hour to his life?" (Matthew 6:27, NIV).

Working full-time all the way through law school sometimes left me with inadequate time for study. I have teased for years that I graduated with lowest honors. As was typical of law schools in that era, it was one course, one final examination, one grade. Period. Roll the dice once and stand by the score. It was good preparation for the rigors of the bar examination and courtroom practice but it was nerve-wracking to say the least. After a passing but less-than-spectacular grade in one course, I remarked to someone at church that I should be the happiest guy in town because Solomon had said that "in much wisdom is much grief and he who increases knowledge increases sorrow" (Ecclesiastes 1:18, KJV). Judging from my score, I had very little wisdom!

Problems somehow become more manageable when we smile at them. It is what they least expect. If an idle mind is the devil's workshop, as our teachers used to tell us, then a laugh and a Bible verse should keep them in their place for another day. Yes, Mom, I remember.

After the Fire, Flowers

Moving forward a quarter century from my own law school days, Marti and I traveled to Lubbock Texas one fine spring weekend to attend the graduation of our son Christopher from Texas Tech Law School. The terrain in west Texas, though monotonous at times, has its own striking beauty, especially in the areas where gently rolling red hills dyed with every shade of wildflower meet the cerulean blue sky of morning.

Cresting a hill, we saw one such scene spread before us like country butter thick on homemade bread. But as we slowed down to feast on the sight, we noticed a stretch of some hundreds, many, many hundreds of acres off in the distance where the Mesquite trees were dead. Closer inspection revealed that a range fire had burned willy-nilly through the countryside, leaving its scars behind. But, curiously, the wildflowers in the burned out area were unusually thick, colorful and splendid. True, the trees were gone but the change in the landscape had its own rare beauty, highlighting the new growth that covered the black-stained earth.

Survivors, too, have their own special quality. Perhaps you have met a hat lady. I have one in mind as I write this story. She is a breast cancer survivor, to be specific, and the hat is her crown of glory. Although she has temporarily lost her hair because of chemotherapy, she wears the hat not only of necessity but as an honor. She is fighting the good fight, a fight for which she will always be known as a victor.

After the fire come the flowers.

Flowers. Hats. Sweet reminders that Our Father dries our tears and makes the end of Job greater than his beginning (Job 42:12). Our horizon at this moment of crisis and conflict may be very low indeed, but the time will soon come when even the eagles will not be able to fly with us. Please emphasize the word "will" in the following passage: "Those who hope in the LORD *will* renew their strength. They *will* soar on wings like eagles; they *will* run and not grow weary, they *will* walk and not be faint" (Isaiah 40:31, NIV). Our Father would not have it any other way.

Chapter 9

JUST A LITTLE LONGER

"Others went out on the sea in ships...They saw the works of the Lord, His wonderful deeds in the deep. For He spoke and stirred up a tempest that lifted high the waves...They cried out to the Lord in their trouble, and He brought them out of their distress. He stilled the storm to a whisper; the waves of the sea were hushed. They were glad when it grew calm, and He guided them to their desired haven." Psalm 107:23-25, 28-30, NIV

"Do not be afraid of sudden fear Nor of the onslaught of the wicked when it comes; For the Lord will be your confidence And will keep your foot from being caught." Proverbs 3:25-26, NASB

It wasn't much of a boat, really. But it looked plenty big on the boat ramp of the lake on a beautiful summer evening when I was about nine years old. It was meant to hold about eight people, as I recall. And dad and I had it all to ourselves. I think he had borrowed it from a friend who was out of town for a few days. Anyway, it was quite a treat to go fishing from a "big boat." The lake was calm as a mill pond and the weather was typical for a north Texas late summer. Around Dallas, the weatherman can take a vacation from about mid-June until after Labor Day. The forecast is always the same: fair and hot. No exceptions for that day appeared to be in store.

How quickly things can change! Dad piloted us a short mile or so from where we had launched, to a group of submerged trees where the big ones were often to be found. Having tied us off, Dad got us fishing in short order. The sunset came a little while later and the action picked up. I don't recall exactly what triggered Dad's attention to the sky but suddenly, in a matter of a very, very few minutes, the stars were gone and the wind had picked up drastically. A sudden thunderstorm was bearing down on us. Running the boat onto the main body of the lake where heavy white cap waves had formed would have taken us to the safety of our family car but would have risked swamping the boat. The tree-infested waters offered no easy path to land. It was time to ride out the storm.

Dad made certain my life jacket was on extra tight. He did what he could to ready the boat, checked our bearings and gave me terse last minute instructions about what to do if we were thrown overboard. It looked like it could come to that. The sky was awfully frightening while the wind made the kind of sounds you hear on disaster movies. Somehow, though, I just could not make myself believe it would be that bad. After all, Dad was in charge. He would get me through. When the storm hit a moment or two later, it was like riding a bucking horse on water. Boy, was it rough! Dad kept telling me to hold on just a little longer. That was the one thing he did not have to worry about! I held on as only a kid can who does not like to swim in the water with snakes (I forgot to mention the cottonmouths, didn't I?). Still, I just knew everything would work out fine because Dad was there.

The storm ended as quickly as it had begun. We bailed some water, checked for damage and eased our way out of the fishing spot, back to the open water and toward home. Once again, it was just another peaceful summer evening. I had always trusted Dad for the day-to-day stuff. And now I knew that even the scary part of life was do-able when Dad was around.

Storms of all kinds are like that. They are fearful both from afar and up close. But Our Father is always there with us, helping us to hold on just a little longer, even when our arms, wits and bank accounts fail us. Even losing all does not mean losing Him. If we have only the poorest of clothing on our backs, somehow He brings us through the bitter storm to a higher place. That is our hope and our confidence. Let's share with one another the ins and outs of holding on during the very worst and darkest moments of life.

Storm Season

Most places in the United States have a propensity for some type of bad weather or natural disasters. If you live in California, you learn to live with earthquakes, the Santa Ana winds with a resultant fire danger, and mudslides when hard rains hit. No one from Kansas or Oklahoma needs to have Tornado Weather explained to him. When the dark, warm, humid sky gets a green tinge to it, it is time to grab a bottle of water, a radio, and to head for a storm shelter. For a New Englander, lake effect snow and nor'easters mean that having those winter supplies laid in makes the days bearable as you wait for power crews to restore electricity and as you dig out of many inches, if not feet, of snow. While you are at it, remember that drought and heat kill more people even than floods. And few parts of the country are immune from a sudden lightning strike which can fry anything in its path.

Storm conditions affect all of us at one time or another. Consider Job. He had everything and then suddenly he was marked with disease, having lost his family and his fortune in one day. At times, we can relate to the sentiment that "man is born to trouble as surely as sparks fly upward" (Job 5:7, NIV). I think I hear you asking, "Why do we have storms, and can we do anything to minimize them?"

Many storms happen to us at random. Others occur in part as a consequence of a choice or series of choices we have made that either were less than wise or because they contributed to placing us in harm's way. Stated another way, were Job's so-called friends correct when they told him that his sin was the reason he had lost everything?

Make no mistake. God can do whatever He wants. But being a loving, righteous God *and Father* means that He "has plans for welfare and not for calamity to give you a future and a hope" (Jeremiah 29:11, NASB). Keep that word "hope" close by, for we will return to it in a few minutes. Our Father does not play Russian-Roulette with His children. *All of Our Father's actions toward us are both purposeful and prospering.* When the random acts of disaster strike, we have not lost His love. Nor does it mean that we are sinners-first-class-of-the-grand-order. Jesus directly addressed this issue: "Or do you suppose that those eighteen on whom the tower of Siloam fell and killed them were worse culprits than all the men who live in Jerusalem? I tell you, no..." (Luke 13:4-5, NASB). Drop, drop quickly, any thought you may have that God has it in for you. It simply is not true. But finish with me the rest of Luke 13, verse 5: "...but unless you repent, you will all likewise perish." If we ignore Our Father's perfect Plan for peace with us through the acceptance of Christ, a tower falling upon us will be the least of our worries come Judgment Day.

Likewise, if we engage in conduct that Our Father prohibits, we should not be surprised if unpleasant consequences overtake us. "Do not be deceived, God is not mocked; for whatever a man sows, this will he also reap" (Galatians 6:7, NASB). During the turbulent years of the savings & loan industry fraud crises of the late 1980s and early 1990s, I worked on cases where the government was attempting to recover monies from those responsible. Without divulging confidential information, I can assure you that financial institution officers, directors, agents and employees really did engage in wild drunken parties and riotous living that would probably have made the Prodigal Son blush for shame. Many of those unhappy souls went to prison while others lost their fleeting fortunes, all because, as we used to say, they had become addicted to OPM, other people's money. For this type of storm, there is only damage control, but it is the most important of all: "flee from the wrath to come" (Luke 3:7, NASB) by accepting Christ as your Lord and Savior.

All of us fall, sometimes spectacularly, sometimes only with a simple but painful "thud." The point is still the same, albeit it on a much easier scale. Sometimes Our Father gives us a pinch to draw our attention back to Him. By the way, did your mother do that to you, like mine used to occasionally do to me, especially if we were in a public place where a backhand across the seat of learning wasn't appropriate? That is the Dad coming out in Our Father. All of us are His kids. And all of us have to be jerked back into place from time to time with a providential thump on the head. "Those whom I love I rebuke and discipline" (Revelation 3:19, NASB). It's no big deal so long as we don't let it become one. Learn the lesson and move on.

A couple of personal stories may help you to better see the picture. When I was a child of not quite six years, a small tornado grazed our home, doing some relatively minor damage. I heard the noise, held on for dear life and then scampered to the window to see the small twister give the neighbor's barn a cartwheel tumble into their pasture. It next hop-scotched across the street to score a direct hit on yet another neighbor's house before moving off into a pasture and out of view. Neither sin nor bad judgment caused the damage all of us suffered. It just happened. And when yet another funnel cloud went over my home when I was 23, the wind and softball-size hail had nothing to do with my spiritual state. Yet while this enormous hail was falling, a few misguided souls ran to their vehicles to try to move them to shelter. The hail was literally coming down in sheets. When the storm ended, we had hail 6-8 inches deep in the street as well as wind damage and flooding. Those who were injured by hail while rescuing their prize cars and trucks also had prize welts and headaches for some time. They did not have to go out in the storm. When they chose to do so, they received the natural consequence of their specific choice in addition to the general consequences of the storm that were shared by all.

Perhaps this story will interest you. While running Dallas's Turtle Creek area one summer lunch hour with a friend, we were caught by a thunder shower. We were debating about turning back when God made up our minds for us. Lightning struck the base of a tree less than thirty feet away. By the way, I can tell you that lightning starts at the ground, moves up and meets the bolt on its way down—I was *that* close. Sometimes Our Father sends a clear, unmistakable warning to stop what we are doing and go another direction. The Bible speaks candidly to a number of moral issues which we should heed without need of a lightning strike to guide us. Use good spiritual and common sense and you will avoid your fair share of bolts from the sky and ice rocks on the head.

Learning to Hold On with Hope and Confidence

There will be times in life where you cannot avoid the storms. Certain of them are inevitable, like death and taxes. More, still, are probable, such as serious illness, relationship discord and financial reversals. At other times, we accept the storm as a price for doing what is right, such as when we take care of elderly family members in our home or when we champion an unpopular cause that is close to Our Father's heart.

Let us now face squarely those toughest of all life's crises. I am talking about issues such as the death of a spouse, child or close family member; an injury that deprives you of your ability to walk or use one or more of your senses; long term illness of someone close to you, especially through Alzheimer's, dementia or cancer; domestic violence and significant mental health problems. Add to the list divorce, criminal charges, lawsuits, sexual and gender identity concerns, financial problems that leave you destitute, the loss of a major job or career and so on. Expand this list to include any major traumatic life event. Place any problem you are having right now that leaves you exasperated and exhausted in this blank: _____. This section is about you and for you, personally.

Get Safe. When strong waves threaten your boat, think personal safety above all else. Protect yourself, your family and your assets. Our Father does not intend that you live under constant threat of physical danger or violence. If you are in an abusive situation, get out! Abusers are not like fine wine. They do not get better with age. Flee with only the clothes on your back if need be but seek a safe harbor immediately. Do this for yourself, your children and for those who love you. Virtually every locale has a place where the abused can find safe and confidential accommodations while they are putting their lives back together. Local law enforcement officials will be happy to assist you. They need to know what has happened because if the abuser is not stopped, his conduct will grow worse and more people will suffer.

When you move out, do so, if possible, while the abuser is gone. Bring along a couple of strong friends, just in case things become tense. Plan your move so that you have changed your bank account and your mail to a new location unknown to the abuser. Change your email, passwords and other forms of personal identification. Avoid leaving a trail through social networking websites. The police or knowing professionals or friends can assist you with the details. Make up your mind and go. It will not be any easier next month or next year than it is right now. Consult an attorney for specific guidance on things like restraining orders, domestic violence reports, divorce proceedings and the like. Remember, if your children or elderly family members have been abused, most states require that you *must report it to law enforcement*. Failure to do so may result in criminal charges being filed against *you*. If you have direct knowledge of either child or senior citizen abuse, even if it is not occurring in your home, you will likely be required to report it as well. Most reports of this nature are highly confidential so you should be protected when you tell the truth about what you know. As always, consult an attorney if you are uncertain what to do.

By seeking safe harbor, you teach your children the most valuable of lessons. Our Father in Heaven takes special care of those who are victims of violence. By your behavior, you tell your children far louder than any words that you love them and will do anything to make certain that their basic needs are met. You also break the generational cycle of violence. Generally, boys who are abused run a greater risk of becoming abusers themselves as they grow up. The delicate emotional and spiritual psyche of the child suffers a recurring backlash from domestic and sexual violence for many years to come. Counseling is absolutely essential for you and your children. There are many low or no-cost alternatives available. Make inquiry through your church, state social services department, law enforcement agency, doctor, attorney or counselor. As Marti in her counseling work has explained many times, it takes only one sane parent for a child to grow up healthy and secure. You must be that one sane parent in time of great crisis.

If illegal activity is taking place in your home or personal space, the same principles apply. Get out *now*. Merely being in a place where known criminal activity is occurring could make you an accessory to the crime. Flee and call the police. If the situation happens at work, tell your supervisor and keep a personal, written record of your discussion or report.

If your home is unsafe due to violence in the city, seek other housing options or protect your premises as best you can with alarm systems and the like. Burglar bars create a risk of being unable to escape if a fire starts or if you need to retreat from your home quickly in an emergency. Again, seek help from someone who knows what to do in your situation. Also consider having a family safety plan for any type of emergency. A local fire department representative or emergency response coordinator can help you.

Keep family members, friends and work colleagues posted on what you are doing. Have a system arranged where they check on you periodically until the danger is past. This is the time to let those who are near and dear to you carry some of the load with you as you work toward a more stable environment. Stay away from any perpetrator unless contact is court ordered or court supervised. Paul tells us that we are to be subject to the governing authorities (Romans 13:1-7). Nowhere is this more important than where our safety and that of our children and our senior family members is concerned.

Get Professional Help. I learned a long time ago that I am not a mechanic. When Marti or I have car problems, we have a trusted repair shop that takes good care of us. Ditto as to health matters. Ditto again as to tax issues. All of us need the professional skills of those whose calling it is to work with our specific problem. We may revere the image of the rugged individualist who is self-reliant in all things. But we know it for the fiction that it is. He who would be a jack-of-all-trades in our complex world today will truly be a master of none.

Finding a good doctor, attorney, CPA, computer specialist, or other technical expert often begins with asking family or friends. Your church may have experience with someone. Ask around. A personal introduction from a satisfied patient or customer often helps ease the way and is a good ice breaker. Or go to the internet. You can easily connect to various websites that provide information about professionals in your area. Call a couple of possible candidates. Ask questions. Are you treated courteously and with respect? Is your call returned promptly, preferably the same day? You will pick up clues quickly. If in doubt, ask someone to help you. *Everyone needs professional help from time to time.* The wise man is the one who quickly seeks good counsel when confronted with a problem that is beyond his knowledge. Marti keeps a file of different persons and firms with which we have had a successful experience. Sometimes we add a name even when we do not need it right then. Cultivate your list of good helpers and when the need arises you will be prepared.

From a professional's perspective, let me add that usually the longer you wait, the worse the prognosis. As one attorney colleague of mine rather crassly observed on one occasion after seeing a badly messed up problem, "I can heal the sick but I can't raise the dead." Do-it-yourself medicine, law, accounting, car repair and the like have made lots of professionals a lot more money than if the individual had called at the first sign of trouble. If you are served with lawsuit papers, call an attorney within 24 hours. If you cough up blood, call a doctor on the spot or go the emergency room. If you smell smoke in your car or home, get out and call for help immediately. He who hesitates is lost.

Seeking professional help should not leave you feeling ashamed. In fact, the reverse is true. Dealing with problems through competent professional assistance speaks volumes about your maturity, wisdom and character. And it should leave you feeling better that your particular matter is in expert hands. *Our confidence is multiplied when we have help in our corner.*

Get Hope. Go first to the Expert of all experts. The Great Physician still makes house calls. Cast all your cares upon Him. Speak to your Savior in the anguish of your heart. Speak to Him out loud, in private. Please, dear one, talk with Him. Jesus is the Lover of your soul, your Lord, your Elder Brother, your Best Friend. Jesus' Heart reaches to the very heart of all that troubles you. "Come to Me, all who are weary and heavy-laden, and I will give you rest" (Matthew 11:28, NASB). Learn the truth of your condition: that you are in need of His care and cannot fare well in life here or in life hereafter without Him. *You* are not hopeless. *Your problem* is not hopeless. If you believe in Him, even if you die, you live because The Resurrection and The Life has gone before you (John 11:25-26).

I do not intend to sound Pollyannaish. Your problems hurt. They go deeply to all that is you. No one can understand them as you do, *except Jesus.* Some of you are facing issues that have forever altered your reality. Life will not be the same again for you. Others have gone without sleep, without needed resources, perhaps for weeks or even months and years on end. Your sadness overwhelms and bludgeons you to a state of existence where simply going through the motions of daily living takes all the energy you have. Like Job, the whirlwind has done its worst to you.

At such moments, we, like children of all ages, cry out, "Father, *do something!*" And Our Father hears us and answers us. He is not afraid of our most difficult questions. Psalm 10 (NIV) begins, "Why, O Lord, do you stand far off? Why do you hide yourself in time of trouble?" Is that a question you have wanted to ask God? Look closely at the answer: "But you, O God, do see trouble and grief; you consider it *to take it in hand*" (Psalm 10:14, NIV, italics added). *Our Father both hears us and acts on our behalf.* He *does* do something when we cry out to Him.

Have you ever felt like your prayers were falling on deaf ears? The writer of Psalm 77 felt the same way. This is what he wrote: "When I was in distress, I sought the Lord; at night I stretched out untiring hands and my soul refused to be comforted....You kept my eyes from closing; I was too troubled to speak....My heart mused and my spirit inquired: 'Will the Lord reject forever? Will He never show His favor again? Has His unfailing love vanished forever? Has His promise failed for all time? Has God forgotten to be merciful? Has He in anger withheld His compassion?'" (Psalm 77:2, 4, 6-9, NIV). Now there is a list of questions that any attorney would be proud to propound in court! Hard questions deserve good answers. This one will help you through any crisis. "Then I thought, 'To this I will appeal: the years of the right hand of the Most High.' I will remember the deeds of the Lord; yes, I will remember your miracles of long ago. I will meditate on all your works and consider all your mighty deeds" (Psalm 77:1-12, NIV).

What Our Father has done before, He will do again. Has He helped you through other trials, storms and conflicts? Of course. He has not changed. He is there for you now and will be there for you next time. When faced with the seemingly hopeless moment, reflect on what God has done for you in days gone by. Make a mental or, better still, a written list of all He has done and is doing for you. You will not be able to complete the list because He has done so much for you that you cannot record it all. He answers our prayers "with awesome deeds of righteousness" (Psalm 65:5, NIV) while bearing our burdens daily (Psalm 68:19). Even our tears and the deepest angst of our soul are recorded by Him (Psalm 55:8). Join the Psalmist and souls of all generations who "cry out to God Most High, to God who fulfills His purpose *for me.* He sends from heaven and saves *me,* rebuking those who hotly pursue *me;* God sends His love and His faithfulness" (Psalm 57:2-3, NIV, italics added).

Our Hope begins and ends in the certainty that "The Lord is close to the brokenhearted and saves those who are crushed in spirit" (Psalm 34:18, NIV). Our hope is a living one, founded on the resurrection of Christ (1 Peter 1:3). The evidence is solid. The outcome is certain. His mighty power, splendor and works speak for themselves (Job 38-41). Everything under Heaven belongs to Him and no one can stand against Him (Job 41:10-11). We echo in our confidence in Our Father the refrain of those saints in heaven and on earth who have fought and who continue to fight the good fight. It only remains for us in time of greatest crisis to "Wait for the Lord; be strong and take heart and wait for the Lord" (Psalm 27:14, NIV).

Tools For Taming Troubles

Every occupation has its own tool kit. In law, we use statutes, cases, and interpretative resources to help us identify applicable law and to apply it to our client's circumstances. We use books and web-based information to guide us in the drafting of court pleadings, briefs, transactional materials and the whole range of legal documents. Experts of all sorts lend their diverse skills to a given case. And for purposes of persuasion and presentation, we will employ just about any visual and auditory technique, process or gizmo available in the market place. If it might help, it is worth trying.

Sorting through the detail of conflict and crisis requires a similar grasp on the resources you have available. You can bear up under the load when you use the right skill, tool or assistant. So let's talk about the practicalities in staying afloat when the waves soar high above you.

Compartmentalization. Your life has many rooms. The crisis in which you are embroiled may affect much of your life but it can be kept at least somewhat in check. Modern fire codes require that large buildings have fire breaks. These barriers help contain a fire and aid in saving the rest of the structure. Ships have bulkheads so that a leak in one area need not sink an entire ship. God has made you with the ability to wall off a part of your life for needful periods of rest and for fruitful work in other areas of your influence.

I often discuss compartmentalization with my clients. A lawsuit may take many months or years to complete. At the end, the client will only have a decision, made by a judge or jury (unless they settle), about this major event that means so much to him. That is all the system is set up to do, to render a decision based upon the applicable rules of law and evidence presented. They may or may not have received "justice" as they perceive it to be. It is both a culture shock and a paradigm shift for most citizens. Those who fare best are those who can say, "This is only a part of my life and I will go on no matter what happens." Attorneys do the same thing. They give each case their best effort for the day. Then they turn off the lights and go home while their client lives with the peculiarities of the legal system, the sometimes shocking cost and the very-slow-then-very-fast pace of the average lawsuit. On rare occasion, I have even refused to accept a client because he was so consumed by his case that he could not maintain any semblance of a life outside of it.

Keep your crisis boxed in as best you are able, otherwise, like a wild beast that escapes its cage, it will do you far more harm than would otherwise be the case.

Isolation Equals Desperation. When I trained for my first marathon, that beastly distance of 26 miles, 385 yards,

I was advised to not go it alone. Every week for four months I ran a training run with a small group of first-timers. All of us wanted to cross the finish line without the use of an ambulance so we listened to the veterans, ran the necessary training miles and kept a close eye on each other. We learned that runners who trained with a group generally fared better than those who chose to be lone wolves, at least for their first marathon. Happily, all of us did well on the big day. I have stayed in touch with several runners from that group over the years. Lasting friendships often form when you share a difficult common experience. And usually, your chances of completing the big challenge increase when you involve others.

Those who work through the issues of addictive behaviors know the risk of isolation. When you get down on yourself, alone by yourself, it is easy to slip off into destructive behavior. *Keep close to others when the going is toughest.* Like fog, crisis limits our vision. Having hands close by to grasp may save you from a painful fall.

De-centering. As we struggle to survive in crisis, we tend to spiral more and more into a self-centered world. When our bodies are fighting to overcome a major or life threatening illness or injury we must certainly be smart about our own needs. But beware! When we think only of self, we are missing the healing power of service. When are you least conscious of your own problems? When you are helping someone else with *his* problems. If you are in crisis because you are a caregiver to someone else whose needs consume you, de-centering from that person carries similar benefits. It is a nice antidote to martyrdom. Help the other person with something simple, like preparing a meal or walking the dog or changing the air filters in the home. Consistently think and do outside of your own world and you will have achieved a service-vacation that gives you a short break while it brightens someone else's day.

Cultivate Listeners. Sometimes our world is so chaotic that nothing much seems to help. Maybe it is time for a chat with a special someone. You know who he or she is. They have a way of lending an ear and a shoulder that fits your mood like a warm sweater. Listeners may be loved ones, close friends, strong church acquaintances, internet pals or a trusted professional. If they have that special gift, they will be with you but will not overpower you. Many listeners are simply gentle, wise souls who know the importance of just being there. When silence fills the room, they enjoy it. When you want to talk, they want you to talk. When you have had enough, they smile, touch your hand or shoulder and gracefully leave. Or they sign off with an email that says they are thinking of you.

What comfort these wonderful saints provide! Blessed are you if you are among those of whom it may be said "they listen well." Do not be surprised if the attentive listener occasionally offers a stunning insight into your crisis. Chances are they are picking up subtle nuances that you cannot see. The Holy Spirit may use them to offer food for thought. It is better than therapy. It is "share-apy." And it goes pretty well with chicken soup.

Self-Sustenance Without Guilt. When crisis develops, you enter into a heightened spiritual, emotional and physical readiness condition. The greater the crisis that grips you, the more acute your response. This is the time in which you *must* take care of yourself. Eat balanced meals if at all possible. Take any medications prescribed for you without fail. Sleep as you have opportunity. Exercise to relieve stress as well as to stay healthy. Stay connected with at least a few significant persons. Pray where possible and keep your Bible handy. Personally, I and many others have found the Psalms to be especially helpful when the storms rattle the windows of life. These essentials should not cause you serious guilt pangs. Remember the first lesson of emergency response: you must have your own protective gear in place before you can help others.

May I suggest that this is the most important time to be kind *to* yourself and patient *with* yourself? Accept the fact that this *is* a tough time. Comfort the child within you as best you can. Let him play where possible. Maybe that means that you force yourself to take a walk or roll around with your dog or cat. Keep the date to go shopping with a friend or hit a few golf balls around the driving range. The important thing is to take breaks where possible, even if it is only for a few moments. Pick up the favorite book and re-read that chapter you enjoy so much. Give yourself things to look forward to every day. Maybe it is something as basic as promising yourself that if you can just get through a certain hard task, you will watch the sunset while enjoying a favorite beverage or snack.

Keep those promises to yourself; otherwise the child within you will lose heart when the successfully completed task goes unrecognized. Consider allowing yourself a particularly special treat when you reach certain milestones on your journey. I can recall a time where just about everything that could go wrong in my life did. Knowing that one particular day would be one of the worst days of my life, I allowed myself to enjoy a Super Bowl party with a close friend after the day was done. Many years later, I still have the sweet memory of a wonderful evening after a day where the bottom fell out. If a small piece of chocolate will occasionally help you hold on a little longer, keep it handy. So long as your reward system is neither immoral, addictive, or foolish based upon your circumstances, you are probably OK with a bit of self-pampering.

Be OK With Doing What You Can. It is not easy being human. I suspect dogs tell each other that it is not easy being a dog. But it is a fact. We are limited creatures, whether we are cats or kangaroos or coffee-drinking *Homo Sapiens*. Sometimes we have to be content with our limits. In crisis as in all aspects of life, some days are more productive than others. Try as we might, we miss our goals, our appointments and even our personal needs from time to time.

Be easy on yourself, especially when in significant crisis. Forgive, accept and, if possible, understand the you that longs for better days. Reduce your expectations, knowing that it is hard to keep your cool when you are in a pressure cooker. I tell runners at the various events I announce that you adjust your goals based upon the course, the weather, your personal conditioning and how you feel that day. Look at today's efforts through the eyes of who you are and what you can do here and now. And remember, as one wise soul has said, only the mediocre are always at their best. Some days will be better than others. When things just do not work out, let go, seek Our Father's ever present grace and allow the day to slip quietly into the softly ebbing flow of eternity's tide as He gently draws you to the place of rest.

Gaining Perspective, Relinquishment and Accepting Process. You are unlike any creation God has ever made. While you share common ground with all humankind, you see and experience things uniquely. So let Our Father work through your crisis based upon His design for you.

When we speak of perspective, we understand that each day, too, is different. That is why we must let go of the past, yet without forgetting its hard-won lessons. Jesus instructed us to not worry about tomorrow. Why? "… for tomorrow will worry about itself. Each day has enough trouble of its own" (Matthew 6:34, NIV). In times of crisis, we, like a good marathon runner, focus on one mile at a time. None of us can digest at one time all the food we need to sustain us for a year. But one bite at a time, we receive the sustenance we need. Work through the troublesome minute, hour and day, allowing Our Father to guide unique you over the unique path before you. Shed tears and shout at the wall when you need to. Perspective and process encompass working through our feelings. God expects as much from us. Just read the Psalms written by David and you will see in them the entire range of human emotion and experience. If David was not shy about expressing himself to Our Father, you, also, may do so with the full assurance that God understands and welcomes your expressions of concern. When you are ready, plan for the future as a good manager but remain flexible to changing times and glorious opportunities, for in every crisis a time comes where we will view our labors from the other side.

Relinquishing our supposed hold on our piece of the world takes some spiritual exercise to accomplish. On the one hand, we want action. Let's get this deal done and move on. But we must be willing to forestay our action and accede to God's plan to act or not act as He deems best.

Accepting process means that we allow God's time and plan to unfold as He directs. Before we try a case, most judges require that the parties mediate their dispute. A mediator, as some of you know from experience, is a neutral who gives his best efforts to helping the parties find a common ground of settlement they can both live with. Sometimes it takes many long hours before any obviously positive results occur during mediation. Statistically, mediation results in a settlement perhaps 80% of the time. So even when things do not appear to be making progress, the mediator and skilled legal counsel will tell those involved to "just give it time." That is process. Just as you cannot judge a book by its cover, you cannot judge the fruit of a crisis until the process is complete. Let it happen. Some flowers unfold slowly, while others need only hours or minutes. Our Father, alone, knows fully what kind of flower you are. Let Him nurture you through the specific plan He has for you, being careful not to judge the result until eternity's sunshine fully reveals the beauty of your blossom.

Laugh a Little. You know how it feels when you hit your funny bone. You grimace and laugh at the same time. Crisis, too, has moments like that. We can empathize with the fella who while watching his car burn up, turns to someone and says, "I *knew* I should not have washed the car today!" There is more than a touch of heroism in the one who, while surveying the remains of his storm-ravaged house, remarks that God apparently decided that the old place needed more than just a new coat of paint!

You can't always reduce catastrophe to a couple of lines for a stand-up comic. But it lies within you to see the small slices of humor in the preposterous events of life. If you want to stab Satan in the gut, laugh at the foibles and follies of crisis. Our Father will cheer you on.

Be Normal Where You Can. When the thunder rolls it is hard to go about your daily routine as though nothing is happening. But it is usually possible to do at least a few things normally. Maybe it is only the trips to the grocery or drugstore or to church that look familiar, but at least it is a part of your world that is mostly the same. Find small enjoyment in the normal and the ordinary. Like cherished heirlooms, you will see in their reflection a promise that life goes on and that you will again have a life you can live with, perhaps a far different one, perhaps even a better one, in the future.

Noetic Transcendence: Gold From Sweat and Tears

A crisis without purpose and meaning is like a car without conveniences. You may get where you need to go but there is no joy either during or after the journey. It is a storm without a rainbow, sorrow without a smile, tears without relief and release. That is not Our Father's plan for His children who go through conflict and crisis. Noetic Transcendence is the counselor's term for the process of taking the bitter pill and turning it into the sweet confection of a positive life experience.

In Noetic Transcendence we see conflict, crisis and tragedy as one of God's means of raising us above the pain, sorrow and exhaustion of the moment. It is a way of taking a bad half volley and stroking it back for a higher good, a good that benefits others and thereby ourselves. When we allow Our Father to have His perfect way with us in crisis and conflict, we join with Him in seeing our crisis as He sees it. He takes our sweat and tears and transforms them into spiritual gold.

The good that results can be far-reaching. The child who suffers unspeakable abuse can grow into an adult who nurtures children and champions the cause of those who face the same road to recovery. From a terrible divorce, a woman can shine light and friendship to those who walk the same thorned path, assuring them that God's provision will sustain them. The man who experiences a close brush with death may choose to live his life with a consciousness of God's intimate presence, while avoiding the fool's gold of a materialistic world. Some will change externally. All will experience a deepening of meaning and purpose through the Living Christ.

Each person who grows through deep conflict and crisis stands prepared to be used by Our Father to respond at any time to those who are experiencing a similar storm. They then go out onto the sea in ships, not for commerce, but to rescue the perishing. And we find that Our Father's will is done not only through others, but through us.

Chapter 10

DANCING WITH YOUR DREAMS

"It has always been my ambition to preach the gospel where Christ was not known, so that I would not be building on someone else's foundation." Romans 15:20, NIV

"Where there is no vision, the people are unrestrained, But happy is he who keeps the law." Proverbs 29:18, NASB

"Delight yourself in the Lord and he will give you the desires of your heart." Psalm 37:4, NIV

"Anyone who listens to my teaching and obeys me is wise, like a person who builds a house on solid rock. Though the rain comes in torrents and the floodwaters rise and the winds beat against that house, it won't collapse, because it is built on rock." Matthew 7:24-25, NLT

Ask a second-grader what she or he wants to be when he grows up and you will likely hear an occupational response. "I want to be a fireman!" "I want to be a nurse, like my mommy!" "I want to be a ballerina!" Money usually has nothing to do with it. Something within the child drives him to a larger purpose, even at the tender age of six or seven or eight.

Our Father asks us the same question: "What do you want to be?" We might answer that we want to be successful in our marriage, family or career. Perhaps we answer more broadly that we want a life that has meaning and purpose. Or maybe we just answer like a kid at grandma's house, "I want some cookies!" Cookies are not necessarily bad but we must decide from whose plate we take them, for the world will load us up with the stuff of lifelong indigestion, a thing that God will never do to us.

Dreams carry with them the idea that they are not merely toys of the moment. Like a dance partner that fits the first time, the dreams worth pursuing blend into every fiber of our being, becoming one with the heavenly chorus from whence they are born. If you have not danced with your dreams, stand up, move towards the dance floor and see what awaits you.

"For Winter's Rains and Ruins Are Over"

Amidst the urgency of daily life, we forget that we are a people of dreams. We love spring, but we seldom walk among its flowers. In part, we have lost the enchantment of the well-conceived dream. To whom is spring most valuable? To him whose life lies buried in deepest winter. Wake up, oh soul!

"For winter's rains and ruins are over
And all the seasons of snows and sins
The days dividing lover from lover
The light that loses, the night that wins.

And time remembered is grief forgotten.
And frosts are slain and flowers begotten.
And in green under-wood and cover
Blossom by blossom, the spring begins."

("Spring," Algernon Swinburne).

Would we know the first stirrings of Eternal Spring? Then by His ever fresh grace, we would enjoy the happiness of those springs that have gone before us. Who among us has not known His quickening power, His temperate mercy, His ravishing kindness? Like David, we long to gaze upon the beauty of the Lord and to seek Him in His habitation (Psalm 27:4). In those days now past, have we not seen His blessings poured out and magnified over and over again? Has our memory so failed us that we cannot recall the fine spring mornings of our youthful days when all life was but a flower garden in which we labored and played with equal pleasure? Return, oh soul, to the haunts of thy fairest days and console thyself with greatest hope that what Our Father has done before, He will do again!

Dreams begin in hope renewed. Storms flee Him as surely as the new leaf returns to the favored tree. And if, dear one, that storm assails you *now*, will not flowers follow in its wake? "The sun will not harm you by day, nor the moon by night" (Psalm 121:6, NIV). Your branches may bend, even break in the winds of the moment, but they are a fleeting thing and you are a child of the King! Rejoice and be glad, for great is your hope! Your root is the Root of Jesse, the Eternal Christ whom no wind can shake! He dreams *and plans* wondrous things for you (Jeremiah 29:11)!

Is not Spring designed by Him for the planting of the seeds of dreams? And what He calls you to plant, will He not water, even with His own tears shed in the Garden of Gethsemane, that you and He *together* might reap a most abundant harvest in His good time? And if the thorns pierce on occasion, are not these, indeed, the "light and momentary troubles" (2 Corinthians 4:17, NIV) that are but the merest of sorrows compared to the exceedingly great riches and rewards we have in Christ Jesus Our Lord?

Dream and dream again! Do so often, do so fully, do so in the Spirit of the Ancient of Days. Let Him ground you in your dreams, for only those that rest in the soil of things eternal will yield eternal fruit. Eat not of the apple of momentary pleasure for there resides the worm that will devour you from the inside out. Look around you and see the horrid sight of the worm at work. He labors not only in the great mansions where great miseries reside but in the humble home where the quest for gain far outweighs the thirst for Living Water. While we all must labor for daily bread, "it is in vain you rise early and stay up late, toiling for food to eat—for He grants sleep to those He loves" (Psalm 127:2, NIV).

In our seasons of despair, we, too, cry out "Has God forgotten to be merciful? Has He in anger withheld His compassion?" But see how clearly the Psalmist answers his own question: "Then I thought, 'To this I will appeal: the years of the right hand of the Most High.' I will remember the deeds of the Lord; yes, I will remember your miracles of long ago. I will meditate on all your works and consider all your mighty deeds" (Psalm 77:10-12, NIV). Our journey to renewed spring brings us to the tiny buds that remind us that His miracles of long ago recur with unceasing regularity. Winter's sleep ends. Life within us awakes refreshed and eager for the song of the robin and the joyful work of His day, a day full of promise and purpose and peace.

Seek First the Lofty Heights

Our dreams begin not at ground zero but at the loftiest mountain tops of our innermost being: "seek ye first the kingdom of God, and His righteousness" (Matthew 6:33, KJV). *Where God and heavenly desire intersect, there germinates the seed of all noble dreams and deeds.*

Even after God had made David King over all Israel, David did not fail to remember his Father in Heaven. "Here I am living in a palace of cedar, while the ark of God remains in a tent," David remarked to Nathan the prophet (2 Samuel 7:2, NIV). From this beginning arose the grand design of the Temple which God allowed to be built through David's son, Solomon. Note carefully the lesson. When we see the Holy unattended, we, like David, cannot take our ease.

Where, we may ask, is the Holy unattended? Where is the hard-pressed widow, the abandoned child, the crippled soul? Where is the one who knows not the kingdom of heaven? Where is the one who lacks refreshment, who is oppressed, discouraged, and downtrodden? Wherever you look, there is need.

The great saints of ages past and present day kept and still keep a watchful eye on the flock around them. To be Christ-centered in our lives means also to be other-centered. Those we revere have not hesitated to give the cup of cold water to the weary soul, or to face the wolf of decadence, greed and injustice with a moral courage born of that same fire that caused David to seek a palace for his King Eternal. Our dreams prosper in relation to our service. Our service prospers in relation to our devotion to Our Father in Heaven. Our devotion to Our Father in Heaven finds practical peace in tending the vineyard plot where we find ourselves on a day-to-day basis.

What, then, of ambition? Does it have a place? Can ambition be reconciled to Our Father's Glory? Indeed, it is *for* Our Father's Glory that we may rightly be ambitious. Jesus expressed it this way: "…let your light shine before men, that they may see your good deeds and praise your Father in heaven" (Matthew 5:16, NIV). If the good deed, motivated out of holy fear and love for Our Father, occurs in public, so be it, for Our Father may be lifted up. If that good deed occurs in secret, so be it, for Our Father sees the private act in equal measure and will reward it (Matthew 6:4).

Ambition does not mock the useful but simple daily toil, or the great dream born of the grandest hope. Stephen, in Acts chapter 6, devoted himself to waiting on tables, yet "…did great wonders and miraculous signs among the people" (Acts 6:8, NIV). Nor did his seemingly simple service disqualify him from the boldest, most conspicuous, action. Read with holy awe Stephen's defense of the Faith in Acts chapter 7, a defense that cost him his life for by his testimony he became the first Christian martyr.

We know that great dreams and deeds inspire others. The poet Longfellow, in a prior age, wrote,

"Lives of great men all remind us,
We can make our lives sublime,

And, departing, leave behind us
Footprints on the sands of time."

("A Psalm of Life," Henry Wadsworth Longfellow).

Let us, then continue on with Stephen's story a moment more. Recall who was present for Stephen's last footsteps: Saul of Tarsus, whom we know as Paul, the Apostle. May we wonder for a moment at the depth of the influence Stephen had on Paul? Paul himself would later become a martyr after witnessing to Caesar in Rome. But before then, Paul took a path that was not that of waiting tables. His ambition was different yet it, too, resulted in a noble end.

Some might be tempted to say that Paul's desire to preach Christ where Christ was not known (Romans 15:20) was the greater ambition. But stop. Do lofty heights of ambition require us to leave all for distant lands? Or may we, in fact, accomplish a needful work in our local sphere of influence? Happy are those who recognize that the lofty heights may be scaled in one's own neighborhood. "Delight yourself in the Lord and He will give you the desire of your heart" (Psalm 37:4, NIV).

Possibility Thinking

It sometimes takes the desperate moment to force us beyond our limits into a different order of thinking. Consider one such story as recorded in Mark 9:14-27. His child could not speak, nor could the child escape the seizures and convulsions that threatened his life. Hearing that Jesus was in the area, the distressed dad brought his son to the disciples in the hope that they could heal him. They could not.

What devastation that devoted dad must have experienced! Fool's gold for a fool's errand. Hope denied and more tears cried. Pain not gain; sorrow not solace. Why dream anymore when all you get is another broken heart? Perhaps this describes where you, dear soul, are at this very moment. Read just a little further. When Jesus arrives, the boy convulses yet again. And the anguished man speaks his heart's desire: "'But if you can do anything, take pity on us and help us.' 'If you can?' said Jesus. 'Everything is possible for him who believes.'" What must dad do? "Immediately the boy's father exclaimed, 'I do believe; help me overcome my unbelief!'" (Mark 9:22-24, NIV).

Possibility thinking begins in the moment we seek release from our unbelief. "…Without faith it is impossible to please God, because anyone who comes to Him must believe that He exists and that He rewards those who earnestly seek Him" (Hebrews 11:6, NIV). Consider the litany of those who dreamed and accomplished greatly because they believed that with God all things are possible. Let your mind reflect upon the stories of Abraham, Moses, Rahab, Gideon, Samuel, David, Daniel, Mary and Joseph, Peter and Andrew, Blind Bartimaeus and the Centurion, each of whom reached out in faith where Our Father's unseen hand beckoned them to follow.

Possibility thinking begins with a greater vision than the near-sighted gaze of the unbeliever, a vision rooted in God's Own Word. The book of Nehemiah tells the story of the rebuilding of the walls of Jerusalem after God exiled the Jewish people for calamitous national sins. But even in exile, Nehemiah remembered that God had promised to deliver his exiled people from the "farthest horizon" if they would confess their sins and turn back to Him (Nehemiah 1:9, NIV). Trusting in that promise, Nehemiah received permission and provision from King Artaxerxes to go forward with his dream. Staying insulated from the Adversary's lightning strikes by being grounded in God's Word helps all who dream. "They are not just idle words for you—they are your life" (Deuteronomy 32:47, NIV). I am not much of a handyman so of necessity I always follow the instructions when I am putting together one of those "easy to assemble" projects. And, wonder of wonders, I usually get it right in the end. A Bible well-worn by its user usually points to one who is successful. When the people strayed from what was right, Nehemiah brought them back to their Standard. Our Bible will do the same with us so that we may complete our own dreams.

Possibility thinking accepts the probability of problems. Nehemiah had no sooner commenced the rebuilding when three local officials began to mock, ridicule and falsely accuse Nehemiah. His reply still encourages us today; "The God of heaven will give us success" (Nehemiah 2:20, NIV). Though the persecution continued, Nehemiah refused to quit. Because Jesus has overcome the world and death, we, too, can face trouble with courage and peace (John 16:33).

Possibility thinking continues in prayer and praise. Amidst increasing ridicule, Nehemiah prayed, "Hear us, O our God, for we are despised..." (Nehemiah 4:4, NIV). The poet Alfred Lord Tennyson wrote that "more things are wrought by prayer than this world dreams of." Those who would succeed in dreams also excel in prayer. Paul encouraged the Thessalonians to "pray without ceasing" (1 Thessalonians 5:17, NASB). Dreams begin, are sustained and end with prayer. We, too, may pray as did Nehemiah, "Now strengthen my hands" (Nehemiah 6:9, NIV). And we, too, must praise "the Lord, the great God" (Nehemiah 8:6).

Possibility thinking does not ignore the practical. When Nehemiah's adversaries plotted to fight against him, Nehemiah continued to pray but he also posted guards, around the clock, to meet the threat. Furthermore, he kept family groups together, alternated men between working and standing guard and required even those who were working on the walls to carry a weapon while they worked (Nehemiah 4:9-18). Details define the dream. Our God is a God of order. All of His natural laws bear continual witness to this point. Indeed, the concept of secular law itself is based upon holy norms so that decent restraint may exist among the people. Only then will a vision have any meaning (Proverbs 29:18). God honored Nehemiah's systematic planning as he led the rebuilding of the walls of Jerusalem. Be assured that godly plans, well-made, will receive His blessing and praise.

Possibility thinking is diligent and preserving. Nehemiah's force never took off their clothes and rested only within the walls they were rebuilding (Nehemiah 4:21-23). In like fashion, we who dream also live with those dreams day and night, keeping our wits and equipment about us in case of need. Nehemiah did not run away, even when he was threatened with death (Nehemiah 6:11). Neither will those whose dreams lie close to the Heart of God.

Possibility thinking is flexible. Nehemiah adapted his plans to changing circumstances many times. When opportunity arose to speak to King Artaxerxes about rebuilding Jerusalem, he uttered a quick prayer and seized the moment (Nehemiah 2:4-5). When the king was favorably inclined, Nehemiah asked for further favor (Nehemiah 2:6-8). When problems arose, he adapted (Nehemiah 4:13, 16-23). If we allow God's Holy Spirit to have His perfect work within us, we will find answers as we need them.

Neither age nor career path matters to possibility thinking. The prophet Samuel was but a youngster when God called him to service. David was the youngest of his family and was tending the flocks when he was anointed King over Israel. Moses was an octogenarian on his second career when he heeded God's call of leadership. Rahab honored God even as a prostitute. The Apostle John had been exiled to Patmos as an old, very old, man when he penned the Revelation. Noah did not know what rain was but he built a great ark. Gideon was threshing wheat when an angel appeared to him, stating, "The Lord is with you, mighty warrior" (Judges 6:12, NIV). We may not be mighty warriors in our own eyes but in God's eyes, those who cast their dreams upon Him are combatants in the first ranks of the heavenly realms.

Possibilities unlimited await us amidst problems untold. To see the possibility is to see Our Father's finger pointing to the dream far above the world's wayward strife. Though we may, for now, only see the entrance to the maze before us, His hand will never let go of ours. Like hot breath on a cool mirror, when our dreams need a bit of polishing now and then, we may count on His hand to clear matters up for us in times of need.

Too Busy to Grow Old

My neighbor Tim has three preschoolers. While taking a break one busy weekday evening from foster parenting a pair of early-elementary kids, I chatted with him about parenting on-the-run. Laughing about all the activities that children today have that we did not have, Tim and I came to the conclusion that when you have kids, you are too busy to ever grow old.

Dreams are like that, too. When we build our dreams on the Solid Rock, we may rightly hope that Our Father will give us the desires of our heart (Psalm 37:4). No dream is too big for Him if we are big enough to trust Him for the answer.

For practical reasons, some dreams may be beyond our reach either now or in the foreseeable future. But that does not mean we should limit ourselves to the ordinary. As a young man, I took the advice of a well-known motivational speaker and prepared a life-list of things I would like to do some day. This "dream list" taught me a lot about myself. I hope you will try it. Do not be concerned about the practicalities as you make the list. That will come later. Start with those things that have been on your heart since your earliest days. For example, I would love to go to the moon someday. I doubt I will get there, but it is still on the list I carry in my mind.

Our Father made the stars. He intends that you reach for them. Never give up your dream of flying to the moon. As my dear Marti put it, when you dance with your dreams you will never be lonely.

Chapter 11

REACHING FOR A FEW GRAINS OF SAND

"This is the message you heard from the beginning: We should love one another....This is how we know what love is: Jesus Christ laid down His life for us....Dear Children, let us not love with words or tongue but with actions and in truth....For God is greater than our hearts and He knows everything." 1 John 3: 11,16,18,20, NIV

"God is love. Whoever lives in love, lives in God and God in him." 1 John 4:16, NIV

Perhaps you have spent a few blissful hours on the beach from time to time. It need not be much of a beach. Most anything will do. A bit of sand, some blue or gray sky, water, birds with their varying cries, warm or cold temperatures to suit you. Maybe you prefer the crowds and colors of a summer boardwalk. Or your tastes may run to lonely, long stretches of sand and rocks, far from the traveled ways of man. Your hands may be empty or you may enjoy the firm feel of a fishing pole or the gentle rocking of an inner tube on soft waves.

Something ethereal happens at that place where water touches sand, where the "boundless deep turns again home," as the poet Tennyson said. We don't usually take time to analyze it. Yet it is worth reflecting upon. Is it the infinite call of a world vastly different from our own that tugs at parts of us we scarcely know exist? Is it, perhaps, the sense that on the beach, we are again as children, exploring dimensions of life and eternity far beyond our daily duties?

Where love is concerned, we are also as children, attempting to grasp the mystery of a beach in a few grains of sand and a bucket of sea water. Over a lifetime or even a small part of it, we may be lifted by great waves to unfathomable heights and set gently on shore or dashed upon the rocks. Our knowledge of love is but a fleeting, fickle thing so it should not surprise us when it handles us roughly from time to time.

Our Father does not intend that we be washed upon the shore, half drowned and badly bruised from any encounter with that which purports to be love. Only imperfect love will hurt us. Yet being the imperfect creatures we are, it is imperfect love with which we contend. It doesn't matter. Our Father, through His Perfect Love, can make us so very much more loving and loveable than we would ever dare dream.

Beginning Within

Love's work begins, first, within us. Nor can it happily affect others until we have learned self-love for Our Father's sake.

Many of us struggle with self-acceptance. We see ourselves as fault-laden and guilt-ridden beings who are not worthy of love or capable of climbing the grander stairs of the heavenly realms. Content to abide in shadows, we muddle through daily affairs and relationships without the glow of conviction that we are loved and cherished beyond all things by Our Father.

What evidence would we have of our value to Him? Seize upon this core truth of all Eternity: Our Father so loved all of us that He sent that which mattered most to Him, His Son Jesus, to bring us into His Heavenly Family. God gave us His Crown Jewel so that we could be crowned with eternal life. Let us not consider, for the moment, the theology of redemption and forgiveness, important though they be. Our reach will not yet go so far. Become more basic still. *In the beginning, God loved us. He still loves us. He will always love us.* Partake of this simplest of all nourishment. Drain the cup. Refill it. Drink again, again and again. When you are sad, return to this Cup. When you are lonely, discouraged, beaten up, "rode hard and put up wet," return to it, for from this Fountain, all waters of happiness flow. Without it, we are easy prey for the evil one. With it, we can rejoice in all circumstances.

When we continually, consciously and practically accept the principle that God's love extends to the me-I-do-not-love, we are ready to begin the life-long process of healthy self-acceptance. When a character flaw overtakes us, we can inwardly smile and say, "Well, God, we are working on that one, aren't we?" When others are harsh with us, we can say, "We all have our issues." When life deals us a hard knock, we can say, "Jesus promised that we would have trouble but He has not deserted me because His Love never changes." When our self image is low, we can say, "I am beautiful to Him." When we fail, we can say, "My Father loves me no less whether I fail or succeed."

Refreshed with the sweet wine of His loving delight in our company, we are able to grow into new forms far beyond ourselves. Greed becomes generosity. A troubled spirit turns into a calm oasis to which others are attracted. A son of thunder changes into a gentle spring shower. A talent for working with one's hands is expanded by God into a gift of service to those whose means do not allow them to repay the favor.

Catch the principle: *What we would do for others, we must first do for ourselves.* Would we be kind? We must first become gentle with our own shortcomings. Would we be hospitable? Let us then welcome His gifts so freely given to us. Would we be patient? Let us allow ourselves the grace to live each day knowing that we are a work in process. Recall a lesson from the safety basics of the airline industry. If those air masks suddenly descend from the ceiling, place your own mask on before helping someone else with his mask. *Until we are secure, we cannot secure others.* Until we are secure that Our Father loves us no matter what baggage we carry, our efforts to help others with their luggage may well cause both of us to stumble.

Taking off the Muffler

Even those of us brought up with perpetual summer-time in our blood enjoy an occasional winter day. Texan that I am, any temperature drop below freezing elicits but one response: put on all the clothing in the closet before heading outdoors. By the time I have piled on t-shirt, flannel shirt, sweatshirt, coat and muffler I am almost bullet proof. Breathing becomes something of a chore to say nothing of doing any worthwhile physical activity. Eventually common sense takes over and I sheepishly admit that I do not really need a muffler or, for that matter, most of what I am hiding underneath.

From time to time we all hide our love under a bushel basket of mufflers. We want to keep our heart for ourselves, sharing but a few degrees of its warmth with others. It is not that we are selfish or self-centered or sinful. We are just cautious, aren't we? We prefer to share our heart a little and a little with those who want us. Seems sensible, doesn't it? Why give a gift to someone who will only throw it on the ground?

And that is where the risk comes in. When we take off the muffler, we are vulnerable to the chill others may choose to inflict upon us. Small wonder, then, that we prefer to stay bundled up tightly rather than loosening our collars. So how do we take the muffler off our heart? How we think about love will determine what we do about it. After all, we commit only to that which matters most to us. Consider, then, love's behavior, for in it we find our own unique reasons to unlock the love within us.

Love waits easily. In love, time does not matter. Within its influence, we cease striving against time and tide for love is eternal. And in matters eternal, Our Father has ordained a different order of living and being. The earthly clock does not, cannot, rule love, for The God Who Is Love may not be measured or limited in any way. It is this gift that He shares with us through love: the capacity, however fragmentary and fleeting, to fly beyond the boundaries of time and space. If it seems strange to think of love in this way, consider that we are ordinarily creatures of limits. We age and constantly feel the effects of time's passage. In fact, we seldom bother to think of it. But where love has its perfect work within us and through us, we experience and share perfect patience because we touch eternity, all because God first loved us.

Love cares and shares. The two cannot be separated any more than faith and works can be separated (James 2:17). To care is to give a part of ourselves by focusing on others. It is completed by the act of sharing. Sharing takes many forms. It may be a passing prayer for a stranded motorist or it may be the more direct act of stopping to change a flat tire for the one who is in distress. We accept that caring and sharing may allow us more freedom in some circumstances than others. My efforts at changing the flat tire would be worth little for my skills do not lie in that way. Conversely, a cell phone call to a local road service is easily within my reach but it may not be possible for us to assist in even a limited way if other responsibilities require our attention. It is a delicate balance: to care and share while keeping to the path where God has placed us. The trick is to recognize the opportunity for unexpected good works while allowing His Spirit to free us from the grind of the moment to experience and share love clothed in work garments.

Love knows when to walk away. Sometimes anger flares when we least expect it. The cooling waters of love will sometimes put the fire to rest. Other times, the fire must burn, even though we wish it would not do so. When that happens, love walks away from the fire, rather than adding more fuel to it.

Love knows when to hand off to others. "The body is a unit, though it is made up of many parts" (1 Corinthians 12:12, NIV). Sometimes we need a "starter" to get matters rolling. Sometimes we need tires to make things run more smoothly and sometimes we need brakes to suddenly stop. Love knows that none of us do all things equally well. There is a time to run with a part of a project and there is a time to hand off to someone else. Love knows the difference and with a chuckle exclaims, "Two heads are always better than one when one of the heads is mine!"

Love spreads the success. Successful churches, businesses and households share a common theme: everyone helps everyone else to do their best. It is the opposite of envy. No one gets left behind because everyone sticks together. The success of one is the success of everyone. To put on a happy face, start by showing envy the door.

Love takes out the garbage. Certain tasks just need doing again and again, even though they are not especially pleasant. Enter love with its work gloves on. This is the non-self-seeking love of which Paul spoke (1 Corinthians 13:5). While we may not relish cleaning windows, sometimes we do so just because the task needs doing. Love does the hard thing, the mundane thing, willingly and cheerfully.

Love does not seek to control. That is another way of saying that love is not selfish. My "control" of others smacks more of benefit to me than to them. Where love is at work, encouragement, compassion and empathy will be found in close company. Others will be free to till their own gardens in their own way where we care less about point-ing out the weeds and more about the beauty of the flow-ers others have placed around us.

Love doesn't need fish stories. As a child, I used to enjoy coming home from a lake outing with dad and boasting to mom about the big fish I caught. Because we were "catch and release" fishermen, I was thankfully spared from pre-senting hard evidence. Mom didn't need the fish stories. She loved me in spite of them and not because of them. Love doesn't need exaggeration or evasion. Love is not for the braggart but for the simple child within us who knows that deception is to love what mud is to mom's clean floor.

Love forgets. All of us have times where we are difficult to be around. Those who love us do more than just over-look those moments. They forget about them. That is what Our Father has done for us. He has forgotten that we are as far from perfect as a cracked pot is from a useful vessel. Because we have trusted in Christ, Our Father has chosen to not only forgive but to forget our bad stuff, even though He is still working to make us what He wants us to be. We touch His Heart and demonstrate that we are His children when we do likewise to those around us.

Love does the difficult thing gently. We must occasionally bear bad news or serve as the discipliner of others. Even here, love is present. Surgeons teach us that the sharp knife cuts the cleanest and with the least amount of pain. Knowing that Our Father deals gently with us, even when He must be severe, we, too, may take some of the sting out of the wounding moment for someone in need.

Love lets go. Among the most difficult of all human discoveries is that some, perhaps many, relationships will not last over the years. Whether we let go at the grave, at the retirement party or at the end of the sports season, we remember that change is inevitable. And if the letting go requires that we give up one who means a very great deal to us, we have the consolation of knowing that by gracefully pulling back, we allow that one to go forward with his journey without the excess baggage of our tormented struggle to hold onto that which no longer exists. Sometimes the very act of letting go in love paves the way for a future reunion. But even where it does not, our heart may claim a great comfort in giving the final ultimate measure of love before we, too, move on.

Love comforts without being superior. When we walk the extra mile with someone who is in need, we share the comfort that we ourselves have received from Our Father (2 Corinthians 1:3-4). Our strength comes from His strength. If we have experience, it is because He has willed it so. If we have words for the moment, it is because He has chosen to speak through us. If we are blessed to fill someone else's need, it is because He has provided us the tools to do so. Consider this profound truth for a moment: God chooses to partner with man. When we comfort others, we share in the partnership, the fellowship, of fellow-feeling and fellow-feeding. And in those moments, we know a little of what it was like to minister with Christ when He walked among the masses.

Love knows where the sunshine lives. If we appear to live in a world of dark days and darker events, we have the joy of knowing that the dark clouds are not the real story. We are children of the King and the world is only a passing wind because we know that He is perpetual light and in

Him there is no darkness (1 John 1:5). That is why love "always protects, always trusts, always hopes, always perseveres" (1 Corinthians 13:7, NIV).

Perhaps you are saying "I can't love like this!" Well, what of it? Just because you are not a gourmet chef doesn't mean you stay away from the kitchen. Just because you are not an all-star, doesn't mean you can't enjoy shooting hoops or tossing the football around. Nowhere is it written that we must be perfect before we can love. Our Father gives us the grace and the privilege to engage in the process of love wherever and however we are at any moment. If we will walk the miles with Him, He will accomplish in increasing measure what we would never dare to dream possible: the creation of a heart in us that is like His own.

Back to the Beach

Along the beach we see many people. A wise man once said, "Remember who you are: we are but visitors in other people's lives." And so it is on all the beaches we visit. Those around us carry within them mysteries we will never fathom. Even those with whom we share the most intimate of relationships still remain fully known only to Our Father. We "know in part," wrote Paul (1 Corinthians 13:12, KJV). Until life here becomes life hereafter we will search love's dimensions equally in part. But it is a part that grows clearer, more wondrous, more beautiful each time we brave the tides and the storms on love's immeasurable beach. And if we explore it only with a child's bucket and shovel, we will still find Our Father there. Amidst those sand castle experiences, He will shape us into that loving creation that can withstand every wave.

Chapter 12

SPIDER WEBS AND GNATS

"So I say, live by the Spirit, and you will not gratify the desires of the sinful nature. For the sinful nature desires what is contrary to the Spirit, and the Spirit what is contrary to the sinful nature. They are in conflict with each other, so that you do not do what you want."
Galatians 5:16-17, NIV

Last Friday was one of those perfect autumn days where the Texas temperatures were mild, the sky a shade of blue that only God could have painted and the air so clear that even the blind could see the far horizon. I went for a lunch-time run to savor those flavors and textures. The local bug population must have had the same idea for in the space of four miles I ran through four spider webs and several swarms of gnats.

The funny thing is, I never saw the first of them. And even after I had pulled the sticky material off of my head and arms twice, I still had trouble spotting the spider webs. I kept thinking, "Surely that is the end of them." Nay, not so.

I did manage to avoid the worst of the next two for I realized that the pitch of the sun was such that they were invisible unless you could hold your head just so where the sun would reflect off of the web. That took a bit of work to do, but it was well worth it.

Need I tell you that I was paying so close attention to potential spider webs that I never saw the first swarm of gnats until I had breathed in a mouthful or two? Then I had to adjust to not one peril but two. So much for a lazy run! It was eyes open and brain fully engaged from that point on. Once God had my attention, He showed me an important parallel. *We seldom see sin until we are trapped within it unless we are focused and willing to allow God's Light to direct us away from evil.*

My experience with spider webs and gnats carries forward to the every day world of jobsites, classrooms, errands and leisure time. *Moral integrity does not just happen.* It must be cultivated by constant, careful attention to all the tools and resources that Our Father has given us. *When we run merrily along without due attention to His Guiding Light, the spider webs, gnats and snakes of life will attack us without mercy.*

Stepping on the Snake

We place ourselves in harm's way all too often and too easily. Perhaps it is the lingering look at an attractive member of the opposite sex that lights a fire which becomes uncontrollable. Or it may be the tendency to share just a little too much of what someone else has told us about the fight between two spouses that leads us into the realm of gossiping, which later forms in us the habit of malicious tale-bearing. We become better at a particular task by repetition. Why do we expect a different result from the labors of old-fashioned sin?

Our subdivision was built in an area of long-standing natural hard wood forest near the site of a Civil War era potter's mill. The plants and critters had reclaimed it before the developer began chipping away at their turf. Not surprisingly, we saw the local inhabitants (skunks, bobcats, deer, scorpions and the like) with some frequency until the community was fully built up. One afternoon, Marti stepped out of the front door, down onto the sidewalk and squarely on top of a snake. It gave Marti quite a shock and the snake writhed in disapproval of its ill treatment. It was not the snake's fault for being there. We had invaded its domain. So it is also when we travel too closely to the boundary lines between sin and good conduct.

We read our horoscopes, joking that what is said in it is pretty ridiculous. But when some pleasant news comes our way, we say with palpable double-mindedness, "My horoscope was right!" Coincidence? Certainly not. Satan acts with a plan and a purpose to take our life, steal our joy and deny us the peace Our Father gives us when we show a willingness to play on the wrong side of the fence. Only when we are deep into his spider's lair will Satan deliver the death poison that destroys our family, our career, our fortune and our good name.

The snake takes many forms, some that we see and some that we do not. When I was a college freshman, I was on my way to biology class one morning when I heard a commotion not far behind me. Looking around, I saw some students gathered around something but I could not tell what it was, so I continued on to class. The professor arrived a few minutes later than usual. Motioning to me, he said that a visitor was following one of the students up the stairs so he invited the visitor to class. He then produced a Bell jar containing a two foot coral snake, that most colorful and deadly of all American reptiles. Sitting up a little straighter in my chair, I memorized his color pattern ("red and yellow will kill a fella"), his dark eyes and what habits I could observe. I have never seen another coral snake. Hopefully, I never will. But if I do, I like to think he will not catch me unawares.

Still, sin finds us all asleep at the wheel time and again. *When we become tired, depressed, lonely, hungry, or prideful, we need extra vigilance and companionship, for the Snake is close at hand.* When He bites, the results include these: "sexual immorality, impure thoughts, eagerness for lustful pleasure, idolatry, participation in demonic activity, hostility, quarreling, jealousy, outbursts of anger, selfish ambition, divisions, the feeling that everyone is wrong except those in your own little group, envy, drunkenness, wild parties, and other kinds of sin" (Galatians 5:19-21, NLT). We can avoid the Snake, but not in our own power nor with our own methods.

Waking the Watchman

"Quick! Catch all the little foxes before they ruin the vineyard of your love", wrote Solomon (Song of Songs 2:15, NLT). *Moral integrity begins with vigilance.* Of what use is a security guard who does not make the rounds, checking all the locks and possible points of entry to make positively certain that no one can enter without the guard's knowledge and approval? Would that same watchman retain his job for long if he allowed pranksters to play in the company parking lot? If he did, what would he next allow? And are we any different? If we cross the line between solid moral conduct into the gray swampy area that is the no-man's land of indecision, we have already allowed the enemy to separate us from our Good Shepherd. The Wolf may be masquerading in any number of forms, but be assured, the warmth you feel is not from The Light of the World but, rather, from the hot breath of the Adversary as he closes in for the kill.

Before we may be vigilant, we must first agree there exists a real, substantial danger that impacts us directly. In my early childhood, my dad's parents had a cotton farm on the High Plains of west Texas. It was dry, dusty, non-irrigated land that looked like something from Steinbeck's *The Grapes of Wrath,* stuff that anyone but a desperate farmer would abandon. But it was rich in adventure to a small boy. I happily helped with what few chores I could, not the least of these being the gathering of eggs from the hen house. I was always cautioned to be careful for snakes and I did pay attention but only in a little boy sort of way. Upon arriving for one visit, my granddad showed me a six-foot diamondback rattlesnake he had killed earlier that day...right in that same chicken coop where I would have been collecting eggs had I arrived only hours sooner. I grew up just a bit that afternoon and I never again entered the chicken yard without all the vigilance I could muster.

The danger to our souls and those of our family, friends and loved ones is infinitely more real and deadly. Until we believe this passionately, we will be under-prepared for the tasks of spiritual survival and leadership.

We must also agree that we are directly responsible to warn those around us. In many legal jurisdictions in America, if we control a home or business premises, we are responsible to warn of known, hidden dangers and to make periodic inspections. That is what a watchman does. Like a military sentry on duty, he keeps a sharp eye out for any and every thing that may pose a threat to those inside the camp. He patrols his given area, reporting faithfully any activity that might be dangerous. In Old Testament times, the watchman who did not warn others was guilty of a sin before God (Ezekiel 33:6).

Nor may a soldier-watchman ever desert his post. He must stay in place until he is relieved by his superiors, otherwise he is subject to a court-martial. The reasoning is plain: all are dependent upon the steadfast attention to duty of the watchman for their security.

We must allow ourselves to be directed entirely by Our Father and His Christ. It begins with our own household and expands outwardly to all with whom we come into contact. Marti and I have adopted as a life-verse this scripture: "Unless the Lord builds the house, its builders labor in vain. Unless the Lord watches over the city, the watchmen stand guard in vain" (Psalm 127:1, NIV).

On that fateful November day in 1963 in my birth city of Dallas, Texas, President Kennedy was to have delivered an address. The words he never lived to speak but that were on his heart included that passage. How important it is to remember that as the household goes, so goes the nation! If we watchmen of our families abdicate our duties, the Lord cannot and will not keep us, our families and our country safe from harm. If we refuse to abide in His counsel, the battle is lost.

As watchmen, we must be attentive to the small, creeping sin as well as to the great moral challenge for if we are faithful with little, we will better prepared to be faithful with much. It starts with the small things we learn as children. Fear God. Tell the truth even when it hurts. Share with those around you. Respect authority, beginning with your parents. Be grateful for what you have. Clean up your own mess. Listen carefully. Learn from those who are wise. Love your family. Help your neighbors. Choose your friends wisely. Read good books. Finish what you start. Smile and be cheerful, for no one likes a grouch.

We practice the daily virtues and then one day Satan dangles The Apple in front of us. What will we do? I remember when my dad met that moment. I was in my late teens and beginning to learn the ways of the world at large. Dad had schooled me well on the importance of personal integrity but I suspect he had no idea when he knotted his tie and went off to work that morning that he would later teach me a lesson that I would cherish for a lifetime, passing it down to succeeding generations. When Dad came in, I *knew* something big had happened at work. Once we were alone, he told me that he had been told he could have a big promotion if he was willing to look the other way on some financial issues. Dad refused, turned in his resignation and went another way with his career.

Well did the poet speak when he said, "Once to every man and nation comes the moment to decide; in the strife of Truth with Falsehood, for the good or evil side" ("The

Present Crisis," James Russell Lowell). The smallest streams of spiritual practice run into the largest rivers of global conduct. As the man goes, so goes mankind.

The little foxes that spoil the grapes become the wolves that devour businesses that destroy the ethical principles and practices of a country that erode the very foundations of civilization. There are no insignificant moral choices; only watchmen who are asleep.

A War Unseen: The Look of Hell

The Baby Boomers became the first generation to grow up with instant access to the world beyond our own neighborhood. Matters that our parents spoke of in hushed tones behind closed doors came to us in shocking reality. When the Cuban Missile Crisis erupted, we knew instantly that the duck-and-cover drills in school and the stock-piled canned and boxed food might save our lives. When man went to the moon, *we* were there for his first steps, like some extra-terrestrial Edward R. Murrow. And we saw the wounded and the dead carried from the forests of Vietnam while we were eating dinner around the television.

The moon and war became physical, tangible reality in a matter of scant years. And then came 9-11, referred to by some as our generation's Pearl Harbor, when our entire concept of war and war's reality changed forever. Our enemy was no longer a soldier in uniform with a face. He was shrouded in a dark culture, without recognizable countenance or military command. His maxims of war made no room for sparing innocent civilians for they were and are his targets. Our gut tightens while our eyes narrow at the word "terrorist," that most hateful of all combatants.

But you know him already. His face is that of the hidden spiritual warfare of which Paul spoke when he said, "For our struggle is not against flesh and blood, but against the rulers, against the powers, against the world forces of this darkness, against the spiritual forces of wickedness in the heavenly places" (Ephesians 6:12, NASB). The greatest war of all time has, from the beginning, been an unseen war. Never doubt that it is real. *Never doubt the fierceness of Satan's struggle for the control of each person.*

I unexpectedly saw The Look of Hell in the flesh one morning in my law office. An elderly man with an advanced, incurable disease came to see me about a personal legal problem. Having learned that for many years his business interests had been in the pornographic trade, I tried to steer the conversation towards Christ. Each time I did so, his very countenance changed. I hardly have words to describe it, except to say that his eyes went as cold as some maniacal serial murderer and his voice took on a steely tone that I have never encountered before or since. "This one is mine," Satan seemed to say. "I have bought and paid for him. His pleasure is my pleasure. You will not rob me of his company!" You will not be surprised when I tell you that the hairs of my neck stood on end while cold sweat formed on my spine. This was The Enemy. I knew his face and he knew mine.

The man wanted no part of Jesus. I wish I could relate a happy ending to the story. In truth, I do not know the ending. I only know I never saw him again as, reportedly, he had only a very few months to live. *Literally*, he had only a few months to live, as he was destined for an eternal separation from God that would have made any earthly existence, no mater how wretched, pleasurable by comparison.

As chilling as this story may be, I wish everyone could see what I saw that morning for then no one would ever doubt that Hell is hellishly real, personal and present in our daily midst. When I was perhaps ten years old, a neighbor whose house was maybe seventy yards from my bedroom window, was working in her front flower bed when a five-foot poisonous snake bit her on the hand. She was a nurse who worked for a prominent physician and even with all the skilled care that was immediately available, she almost died. I had walked past that flower bed many times as had her grandchildren who were my friends. That snake could have been there at any time and could have bitten any one of us.

Our family, loved ones, friends, work colleagues, classmates and neighborhood acquaintances depend upon us to take our part in the Great Spiritual War against the Serpent. Of those dear souls, many have no idea they are in danger of snake-bite or if they do, they think a spiritual band-aid will take care of any wound. You know otherwise. The Enemy is as near as the next temptation.

Fighting Back

Only when we accept the stark spiritual reality that we are each fighting an unseen war whose effects litter our jails, courts and communities with brokenness, can we fight back with the multitude of spiritual weapons available to us. That is why Paul instructs us to live by the Spirit.

Jesus left His disciples to return to Heaven until the time appointed by Our Father for Him to return to us again. But Our Father did not leave them or us without His Presence. If you, like many, do not quite know what to make of that Third Person of The Holy Trinity, God's Holy Spirit, take to heart three central things He does for us. Jesus told His disciples on that last, holy night, "the Counselor, the Holy Spirit, whom the Father will send in my name, will teach you all things and will remind you of everything I have said to you" (John 14:26, NIV). Note carefully the verbs "teach" and "remind." Now add the third verb, "guide": "But when the Spirit of truth comes, he will guide you into all truth" (John 16:13, NIV).

Teach, remind, guide: in these three ways, Our Father's Holy Spirit continually assists us. He never leaves our side. He always touches our conscience with that which will lead us through the momentary and the long-term crisis. His wisdom is perfect because it is of and from Our Father. He does not require payment because He is a gift. When you consult an attorney, you are at the mercy of that counselor's personal education, training, experience and goodwill. With the best intentions, your attorney will never know you or the facts of your case perfectly. Your attorney is a substitute warrior who, at the end of the day, will go home to his own concerns, leaving yours behind. That is not a criticism. It is merely an objective statement of the process.

Oh, how wondrous is Our Father's care for us! Day and night we may lift up our cares and petitions to Him, knowing He ever hears, ever cares, is ever there! He works us though the progression of His grace with teaching from

His Word and with direct assistance in understanding and applying His teachings, with the personal counsel of the Holy Spirit. He reminds us of what we have learned and of what we need to recall through that same wonderful Friend who literally takes us by our spiritual arm, guiding us away from the snakes and gnats.

Speaking specifically, how does Our Father teach, remind and guide us? Here we could fill many a book with the testimonies of those who have experienced his care. The witness of those who know Christ will give you far more information (and praise!) than I could ever offer here. So let me present just a few general observations.

First, those who are of His flock know His voice more surely than any other. Jesus said, "I am the good shepherd; I know my sheep and my sheep know me—just as the Father knows me and I know the Father..." (John 10:14-15, NIV). Speaking of His flock, Jesus assures us, "But they will never follow a stranger; in fact they will run away from him because they do not recognize a stranger's voice" (John 10:5, NIV). We know Jesus' voice the same way Jesus knows Our Father's voice. Consider how readily a mother knows the cry of her own child. Or ponder the miracle of how the mother of a baby penguin distinguishes that one voice above hundreds of others. It *is* a mystery. But it exists nonetheless.

He teaches, reminds and guides us through His recorded Word, he Bible. Our Father will not act inconsistently with what He has already told us. If the Bible gives specific instruction that we are not to steal, then we need not inquire whether we may take anything that is not ours. Now expand the concept to your daily affairs. The Holy Spirit will help you see how to address an employer who asks you to do something that may be morally or legally wrong. For instance, you may not sign a report containing financial information that is incorrect as it may be both criminally wrong as well as morally repugnant. Simultaneously, Our Father may give you an opportunity to share with your superiors the reasons for your conduct. Aside from giving glory to God, it may also keep you out of jail or a lawsuit, even if you are fired as a result of your refusal to compromise. In that refusal, Our Father has guided you out of the larger storm and He will, just as surely, make a way that is better for you.

Occasionally it is through the wise counsel of others who also hear Him that Our Father's Holy Spirit leads us down "the paths of righteousness for His name's sake" (Psalm 23:3, KJV). I like how the New Living Translation renders Proverbs 19:20: "Get all the advice and instruction you can, and be wise the rest of your life." Psalm 1 comforts us with the knowledge that the person who does not walk in the ways of evil counsel, but whose delight is in God's Law will "yield its fruit in season," his "leaf will not wither" and "whatever he does will prosper" (Psalm 1:3, NIV). Even if the circumstances of the moment are bad, the end result of your life will be a lasting legacy celebrated in the Heavenly realms.

Our Father will use circumstances to direct you, for He holds all matters in His power. Sometimes, you will be the one served, as I was once in law school. That first year, I was so poor that even the church mice saved cheese for our family. A kind soul, the identity of whom I never discovered, left a sum of money in my mailbox that tided my family over for some weeks. Other times, He may call upon you to put your time, talent and treasure to use for His special calling. Sometimes, He will delay or expedite events according to His timing for you. Allow Our Father to open each of His flowers for you in His own good time. And when trouble comes, know that He will bring about a resolution that leads you to higher ground.

Captive Thoughts: The Key to Spider Web & Gnat Control

Return to the days of the Corinthian church, which dwelled at the crossroads of the greatest trade routes and human knowledge of the day. Like today's society, new ideas and great human degradation coexisted in a cosmopolitan society that challenged the upstart Christian church to declare itself relevant. What secret of success did Paul share with these fledglings who existed in the sea of worldly temptation and contradiction? "We demolish arguments and every pretension that sets itself up against the knowledge of God, and *we take captive every thought to make it obedient to Christ*" (2 Corinthians 10:5, NIV, italics added).

Take every thought captive. Leave no weeds in which the Snake can hide. Stand watch over everything you allow inside your spirit, knowing that you do not do so alone or in your own power. Our Father's very own Spirit serves you so that you may catch the small sins and the great before they lay ruin to all you hold dear. Only in His Light will you see the unseen and un-seeable spider webs and gnats so that you may fight your way through to the Heavenly places.

Chapter 13

STRAIGHTENING THE ROOM

"All Scripture is inspired by God and is useful to teach us what is true and to make us realize what is wrong in our lives. It straightens us out and teaches us to do what is right. It is God's way of preparing us in every way, fully equipped for every good thing God wants us to do." 2 Timothy 3:16-17, NLT

Do you sometimes look around your home or work-space and realize that things have become too messy? I have kidded Marti for years that we guys do not have the same "clean gene" possessed by our ladies. Generally, if it isn't growing mold, it is clean enough for me. OK, sometimes I don't bother with it if it *is* growing mold. Maybe I am exaggerating a little, but moms look at dirt differently. Clothes scattered around the room, an unmade bed and dirty dishes on the dresser usually evoke a sharp response from the female parental unit to wake up, shape up and clean up *right now*.

Truth be told, I feel rather lost when I cannot find my way around an office that has become layered with the alternating fossilized strata of books, files, technology paraphernalia and miscellaneous paper. Our spiritual life is no different. A certain amount of structure helps us make sense of the whole, keeping us in order so that we may function as Christians without duplicity. Our standard of wellness and orderliness is the Bible. And it is Our Father who calls our attention to this important piece of spiritual housekeeping.

We need not fear His cleansing power; quite the opposite, in fact. Like a warm bath or shower at the start or end of a busy day, His word reaches deep to the tired, sleepy muscles, soothing and renewing them for the road ahead. Sometimes we need a vigorous massage to shake us up and get us moving. Scripture provides just the right touch. Sometimes we lack information with which to make a decision. Enter the pages of Holy Writ to find your way in those moments. Whatever the need, whatever the sorrow or joy or perplexity of the hour, Our Father has already prepared the way. You need only open The Book to find direction.

The Renewed Joy of Discovery

Somewhere along the path of learning, we have misplaced a core truth: learning should be more about pleasure than pain. Certainly, our definition of "fun" must change as we put away childhood. But we will be poor indeed, no matter what our balance sheet says, unless we retain the child-like thrill of discovery.

Last night at the local bookstore, I heard a storyteller, one whose gift is the transmission of great tales and legends from one generation to the next. Through words and primitive cultural music, we were drawn into a different world, one far removed from the hassles of Christmas shopping and daily chores. I am not certain that any of us wanted to let go, to come back to the present moment. For an instant, we were all children again, sitting at the feet of one who understood the mysterious and who was leading us by the hand into old, beautiful truths.

My Bible this morning is the same battered and bruised friend that it was last night. Now and again, I recognize a grease-spattered page or a particular emphasis I placed on a marked passage that spoke intimately to me at a needful moment. I have regained a lost perspective overnight. It is more than a book, more than a story. It is my heritage, the sum and substance of all that has gone before me, the foundation upon which I build either worthily or unworthily. It is the story of the journey, triumphs and setbacks of all that is humankind, past, present and eternal, seen through the eyes of those great story-tellers who spoke as Our Father gave them utterance. We call it the "Holy" Bible for a reason: because it is set apart from all other literary works as a source of all that will endure when all else fails. Today, that is my first, renewed discovery.

Our Father bids us sit at His Feet to hear anew the glorious, poignant, breath-catching, and heart-stopping tales of adventure, intrigue, romance and beauty that He has recorded for all His children. This is not some magician's magic-wand-of-an-invented-world from which we experience a few passing moments of quickly forgotten pleasure. Fantasy stories abound in our present age, no doubt because of our universal desire to escape the mundane and the troubling, sometimes senseless, world around us. And pleasant it is for the moment. But we return to the old world yet. We are still wetted by our own tears, drunk on the poison of discouragement and disease mental, physical and spiritual.

Not so in the Land of the King. Look at Elijah, in front of wicked King Ahab and the lost sheep of Israel, confronting the prophets of Baal, laughing at their pathetic attempts to call down fire from heaven through a god who is not there. Notice the silence as he rebuilds the Altar of the Living God, one large stone at a time. Experience His deep reverence as he enters the holy moment of prayer. Shout with all your might the victory of the Fire That Answered! You, too, are made to be a hero! David's confidence before Goliath lives in you for you are made in Our Father's Image, just as Elijah was. In you runs the strength of Elijah to lead others to The Only God. Through you, like Rachel, a great love cries out, "Give me children, or else I die!" (Genesis 30:1, KJV). See before you the spiritual offspring who await you when you share His Word with them.

This day, this moment, discover who you are in the pages of Holy Writ. Abraham saw your star when The Sovereign Lord called him to look up to the heavens and told him "So shall your offspring be" (Genesis 15:5, NIV). Your time is today; your moment is a part of the victory tapestry on display in the heavenly realms.

Behind the Scenes

In the early days of cable television, my home church presented a weekly affairs television program on a small local channel. When I was asked to host it, I quickly agreed.

Hollywood at last! I could hardly wait for my first program. Please understand that this was not Tinseltown, glamorous celebrities and a cast of thousands. Our studio was a small set at the local junior college. Our production staff consisted of a few technically-minded volunteers. Our guests were not paid; our sets were not Broadway quality. But we made do and in fact I like to think we did rather well. Because we were not given much time, every minute in the studio had to count. That is where I learned that a very great deal of preparation occurs behind the scenes in advance of the cue to roll 'em. Before the mystery of the magician or the interesting conversation with a witty, learned guest, all concerned had laid the cables, checked and re-checked the equipment, positioned lights, endured makeup and researched the subject matter of the show from every possible angle.

It all looks so easy on TV, doesn't it? In fact, any great work by anyone, viewed from a distance, usually appears to be flawlessly and seamlessly executed. Of course we know why it is so. It is all in the preparation. The devil is not in the detail: he is in *not doing* the detail. Even with the preparation, curious, strange things can happen. The trick to a fast recovery is all in the collective experience and diligence of those who are front and center.

We all carry with us certain personal maxims or wise sayings to help us when it is our time to show the crowd what we have. The craftsman may recall the instruction to "measure twice and cut once" while the athlete may remind himself that "the pride lasts longer than the pain." Or how about "be specific about being general," a standing commandment for writers and speakers I learned through a venerable high school English teacher? And here is one we have all heard many times: "practice makes perfect."

What we practice often, we often become. Somewhere along the way, behind the scenes, we acquire the skills that enable us to function in the world. Use makes master, as the experienced tell us. We may not remember when we learned how to open a door but we can easily recall opening the door of our first place of employment, our first motor vehicle or our first apartment. It is no small miracle that we have acquired untold thousands of skill sets, each through varying degrees of study and repetition. "That is no big deal," you might be thinking. Tell that to a child who has just mastered his multiplication tables! For the kid who loves numbers, basic arithmetic may lead on to elementary algebra and then to geometry, trigonometry, calculus and a career in engineering, actuarial science or that of teaching in a school classroom where the next generation awaits the passing along of the progression of knowledge.

If we would become Christ-like, if we would *know* Christ, we will privately, behind the scenes, practice the putting on of Christ. We put on Christ by studying Our Father's Word and by applying what He teaches us. Those few minutes of daily Bible study, the evening moments of bedtime prayer, cultivate in us a sense of devotion to Our Father. From devotion, we acquire an increasing measure of the conscious presence of Christ in all that we do and an increased faith that He will act on our behalf. Our habits begin to conform to a heavenly standard as we take "every thought captive to the obedience of Christ" (2 Corinthians 10:5, NASB). Study, practice and experience lead us ever to higher ground.

Becoming What We Grasp

Do you play a musical instrument or do you work with a particular favorite tool? How did you learn its secrets? You picked it up and played with it. A guitar sitting in my hands is just a wooden box with strings but in the hands of a maestro, it is a world of glorious sound unto itself. Our Father has created a spiritual language with eternal notes that may be played even by a beginner, but first we must learn to read the score.

Scripture makes us think. When we study to show ourselves approved before God, we engage in the holiest of all exercise as we stretch our roots and our spiritual limbs ever deeper into the pure soil of his Word.

We are designed and intended for a larger world. Some few years back, Marti and I had a small Norfolk Pine that was in a cramped ceramic coffee pot. Roots and all it was not a foot tall. After disentangling it from its container, I moved it to a larger pot and fed it with root stimulator. Weekly I watered it, making certain it had some sunshine and an occasional round of fertilizer. Now, some nine years later, it dominates our living room! That mere sprout has grown to an eight-foot indoor giant all because of a little attention here and there.

When we dig into our Bibles regularly, we also will grow into fantastic shapes and dimensions. Our problem is not that we are small or that we are not good at Bible study. Our problem is that our container is too small. We are meant for eternity (Ecclesiastes 3:11)! Jump out of that pot that the world has placed you in. Our Father has much bigger things in store for you if you will but think on the things that are more excellent.

We cannot become what we do not grasp. Taking a grip on ourselves requires reaching for Living Water. In many parts of the country we winterize our motor vehicles by flushing the old antifreeze out of the radiator and cooling system. This involves both draining it to reduce the sludge and filling it with new antifreeze. Or take a different example. Perhaps you have a fountain or birdbath in your yard. If you want to clean it out, you can either put your hands into the midst of all the junk (ugh!) or you can take the garden hose and spray in new water that forces out the old. In a short while, the new has replaced the old and you never even had to get your hands dirty. *Put in the new to force out the old.*

It is always easier to get rid of an old bad habit by substituting something better in its place. All it requires is grasping the new. How do we become more like Jesus? By placing His words and those of Our Father in our hearts where, over time, they will loosen the old junk of our former lives and provide us, instead, with new life.

By the way, it does not take much effort to see results. A scant ten minutes of daily Bible time or a few minutes of listening to a quality Bible teaching ministry on the radio or CD player will add up to over 50 hours a year, not including time in church. Think about it. That is the rough equivalent of a short college course each year. And those years add up in a hurry.

Let me share with you one more story. We planted a Myrtle bush outside our bedroom window. It was only about five or six feet tall and a couple of feet around when we planted it. Unbeknownst to me, our lawn sprinkler system developed a small water leak where we planted the myrtle. We could not even detect the leak from the water bill. In less than four years time, Hulk, as we affectionately call him, grew to a height of 15 to 20 feet with a girth akin to that of the defensive line of a professional football team. All it took was little extra water every day. Want to be a spiritual Hulk? It only takes a little Living Water every day.

Build your own tool box. I am not a handyman. My running joke over the years has been that when I open the tool box, the family yells "INCOMING!" and runs for cover. But it hasn't stopped me from building my own Bible tool box.

It's easy. First, have a Bible that you are not afraid to mark up and wear out. I have an old beat-up Bible that accompanied me through many a business trip. It is falling apart and now retired but I still pick it up once in a while, for a major part of my personal journey occurred with that dear friend. It is *the* Bible I first used for daily Bible time and, like my myrtle-friend Hulk, I grew noticeably from interaction with its pages.

Next, mark those passages and words that grip you. Remember, this is your personal Bible-Workbook so it's perfectly proper to scribble all over it. Let the Holy Spirit coax you through the challenging passages. Take down notes from sermons, Christian books, and incorporate your own thoughts and life experiences. Write it down. Keep a small scratch pad handy in your Bible, if you choose. When Our Father reveals a truth to you, record it wherever you are and whatever time it is. Tuck that thought away in the back of your mind, coming back to it for a moment now and then. Refresh yourself with those passages and ideas that touch you, knowing that you are gaining ground every time you do so.

Develop your own inner or written list of particular Bible verses that help you. Mark them in red ink if you choose in your Bible but keep them handy. Like the feel of a solid tool in your hand, you will take comfort in their particular ability to assist you with the task at hand. And they will keep you balanced when your world moves in a difficult direction. You will also be able to find them more quickly when the need arises.

Invest in a few Bible tools. Any good Christian bookstore can help you. I keep a concordance near by where I can find that verse that I partially remember. You need only know a key word or two to locate that half-remembered passage. A Bible dictionary or handbook will also help bring the landscape of Scripture into focus. If you like words, try a book that explains in more detail the origin and meaning of the words used in the original languages of the Bible. Keep a set of maps handy (many Bibles contain an adequate set near the back pages). Explore the life and times of the different persons and places you encounter. Have fun at the bookstore and at online retailers where affordable resources await you in both traditional and digital media.

Oh, by the way, if someone yells "incoming!" your Bible can be a pretty effective shield from someone else's slip up.

Loving Him More Than These

Did you ever play dress up as a child? Maybe you "downloaded" some tools from dad's workshop, dressed like a favorite character or appropriated the kitchen for a nine-year-old's version of cooking 101. That early bit of make-believe may have helped you think about what you wanted to be (or did not want to be!) when you grew up.

Simon Peter faced a moment where he, too, had to decide what he wanted to be when he grew up. He had followed Jesus for three years, having left behind his fishing gear. He walked the walk with Jesus. He even talked the talk, having announced that Jesus was the Son of God. But then he fell and fell hard, publicly, before Jesus, right down on his spiritual face, when he denied Jesus the night of Jesus' betrayal.

Peter was not Judas. He toughed it out. After the resurrection, Jesus personally took embattled Peter and asked him, "Simon, son of John, *do you truly love me more than these?*" (John 21:15, NIV, emphasis added). When, like Peter, we respond that we love Him more than all else, we will grow up loving and seeking out Our Father's Words.

Chapter 14

WHEN PANDEMONIUM REIGNS

"I do not concern myself with great matters or things too wonderful for me. But I have stilled and quieted my soul; like a weaned child with its mother, like a weaned child is my soul within me." Psalm 131:1-2, NIV

"Lord, you have been our dwelling place throughout all generations. Before the mountains were born or you brought forth the earth and the world, from everlasting to everlasting you are God." Psalm 90:1-2, NIV

That Sunday morning was meant to be a relaxing spiritual journey. We had no plans for the day, no responsibilities, no list of "must do these." We had anticipated our early morning visit to a particular famous mega-church with much delight, savoring the coming experience as one might savor the aromas of a bustling kitchen on Thanksgiving morning.

Then pandemonium struck. *Pandemonium is the condition that occurs when too many pots boil at the same time.* You will recognize it without any further definition. In our case, the dogs had issues, my home-office printer would not work, we woke up a trifle later than we had planned, the car was a bit fractious in starting and small problems quickly spiraled out of proportion.

I am happy to report that none of those problems required intervention by the United Nations. Nor did any paparazzi follow us. I doubt that the President was informed and we were not called before any Senate sub-committee to explain what occurred. We even made it to church on time (sans breakfast, however, until later in the morning) where we reveled in the teaching, music and fellowship. But on my part, it took some hard work to calm myself to the point that I could get on with the day's activities despite the hectic start.

Taking charge of ourselves when pandemonium reigns can be as difficult as it is essential. When we make our way through the canyon of chaos we will find ourselves in possession of spiritual resources that may be reused again and again, without any loss. In fact, those resources will accumulate interest as we put them to more frequent and greater use.

I And My Gardener are One

In recent weeks, our area of Texas has seen more than its share of windy conditions. Because of the way our house is positioned, we catch more wind than the average structure. So we have learned to stake our plants, remove objects that may be blown around easily and shelter the outdoor essentials as much as possible. Still, I have become an expert at chasing our trash cans down the street.

One sunny winter morning, I remarked to Marti that the back yard had lost some of its charm, due to all the debris kicked up by a 40+ mile per hour windstorm. As if in response, the organizer within me seemed to say, "Well, is the gardener on vacation?" I chuckled with the realization that I and my gardener are one. So I donned the old clothes and spent the rest of the day making things tidy again. Even though my back ached and my fingers showed the small blood spots of encounters with thorns and sharp-edged leaves, I ended the day far happier than I started it.

Who was the wise soul who said "Work fascinates me. I can sit and look at it for hours"? Now there is a person with whom I can relate! *When faced with daunting tasks, inertia doth make cowards of us all from time to time.* Some days, we just cannot shift our personal vehicle out of first gear. Perhaps fatigue or frustration or lack of knowledge or experience plays a part in our malaise. Inertia evolves into despair and quick as a March wind, we are blown off course, right into the Adversary's playground.

Moving away from recess with the devil takes a bit of doing. First, we must accept that we are responsible for our own garden. No one makes us rise up for work in the morning but us. Our alarm can bark its shrill call until it runs out of energy but it cannot force us to do our due. Sometimes, we must give ourselves a shove before we can grab the shovel.

Humor helps. Once I began to laugh at my outlook on the backyard, I found it oh, so much easier to confront the challenge before me.

Companionship helps. Marti cheerfully aided and abetted me in my design to clean up this town one leaf at a time.

Perspective helps. Looking at all the work (and the "lost" easy weekend day that would result) before me, I took consolation in the old maxim that "the pride lasts longer than the pain."

Taking the first step helps. By *immediately* retreating to my closet and changing into work clothes, I assumed the role of gardener-extraordinaire. How could I, then, have not picked up my tools and started work?

Focusing on one small step at a time helps. I then picked out the tools and supplies I would need, surveyed the field of battle and placed the first handful of leaves into the bag.

Concentrating on just what is before you helps. If I had worried about "how will I ever get all this done?" I would still be looking at a messy back yard. Eat that elephant in small bites. It is much easier to swallow.

It helps to get help when you need it. I am not the fount of all wisdom. Most clients have heard me say that "two heads are always better than one when one of the heads is mine." It is not an excuse for passing the buck. Rather, it is an acknowledgement that I, alone, am not as effective as when I stand with others, drawing upon their experience, knowledge and wisdom.

Not being concerned about doing everything today helps. One does not build a house, nor landscape and beautify a backyard or a life, in a day. Consistent, small steps yield far greater returns than the occasional giant leap (which often never occurs anyway).

When we accept the truth that we are responsible for our own happiness, our own good humor and our own success, we will have taken great strides to becoming the peaceful person who draws others close in times of conflict and crisis.

Leaving The Important Decisions To God

While taking an undergraduate course in business management one summer many years ago, I chanced to draw a group of classmates without a single female in the lot. Our professor used that rare environment to share some hard-won secrets with us guys, probably in the hopes that it would save our wives some trouble in training us correctly. One day the Professor lectured us about how top management decisions are made. And then he turned to the home front. "Gentlemen," I recall him intoning, "around my house we have an excellent management system which I will share with you. My wife lets me make all the important decisions—who should win the next election, what we should do about national debt, how best we can achieve world peace. She assists me by making all the minor decisions—when we should buy the new car, how much we should spend on the new drapes, where we should go on our next vacation. It is a perfect division of labor!"

He made a pretty good point, didn't he? God knows and I know that He should make the big decisions. I really don't do all that good a job with even the small ones. When David wrote Psalm 131, he probably did not have this example in mind but I suspect he would approve of the sentiment. We are all better off when we concern ourselves less with the great matters, leaving those in Our Father's own hands.

Paying attention less to the bad news of the evening media reports allows us to demonstrate a faith that glorifies God and brings us peace. *We quiet ourselves by hearing Our Father's voice above that of the world.* He speaks to us in His Word and through the gentle, and even the harsh, reminders He places in our path. When we turn to Him to speak His name in praise, to ponder upon some Scripture verse, to stand in awe at some aspect of His creation, to wait upon Him in the uncertain moment, we show that we are the mature child who has been weaned from the spiritual bottle of constant self-attention.

We will likely never be in a position to influence grand political affairs. But Our Father can use each of us to provide safe harbor to some struggling soul most days, even if it is only for a few moments. The small task performed well shines like a pearl on a dark ocean floor. If you are afraid that you will not measure up to the standards of Mother Theresa, remember that she made her way among the wretched masses by offering simple, human-needs assistance, one soul at a time. The child you faithfully attend every day counts. The schoolmate who uses you for a sounding board counts. The boss whom you serve with your best efforts counts. The sports team, the hospital visit, the telephone call or email to one who is undergoing hardship, all count. *Service to others always counts, for in it we cast off self, preferring instead the cross of Christ to individual interest.* In doing so, we quiet ourselves by harkening to the cries of others, becoming in the process instruments of His Peace to those in need.

What a world of joy awaits us! Dear one, does it strike you, as it does me, as a thing too amazing to grasp, that Our Father grants to each of us the privilege of ministry? By what grace does He allow us, nay, lead us, into His world of service? Consider it for just a moment: our hands are *His* hands, our feet *His* feet. When we softly tread into the space of another, bearing only Our Father's good will, we have touched eternity. The 19th century poet Emily Dickinson said it well:

> If I can stop one heart from breaking,
> I shall not live in vain;
> If I can ease one life the aching,
> Or cool one pain,
> Or help one fainting robin
> Unto his nest again,
> I shall not live in vain.

When we quiet ourselves, we hear in our soul even the smallest whisper of need. Nor should we wonder why, for we are close to Our Father's heartbeat.

As we quiet ourselves, we learn what it is to dwell with Our Father. No need goes unmet, given time and an attentive, expectant, patient hope in Him. What He intends for us will surely know our face in His good time. No pleasure can be sweeter than seeing Our Father's Will come to pass, despite the vagaries of a self-centered world. Where He Is, there is no night, no fear, no want. A recognition that the Kingdom of God dwells within us will bring blessed release from those concerns that trouble so many while opening the pantry door of our spirit to the hunger and thirst of others.

Taking Care of Ourselves When God Swirls the Salt

You may remember this simple science experiment. Take a glass of water. Place in it a tablespoon of salt. Agitate the water by swirling it or stirring it. The salt will totally dissolve within the water in a very short time. Our Father sometimes shakes the glass hard indeed. When we are the salt being swirled, it can be difficult to retain our equilibrium while God is dissolving us into His plan. During those times we must be sensitive to the need to take care of ourselves.

When David said that he had "stilled and quieted his soul," we may infer that he took self-help steps to keep his balance. Occasionally, we must tend to personal needs so that we may be useful as salt-of-the-earth and leaven-in-the-bread. When you are legitimately ill, seek help from a qualified physician as well as from the Great Physician. When you are weary to the bone, catch up on your sleep so that you may function efficiently in the arena where God has placed you. Take a lesson from Elijah. When he was discouraged and tired, God fed Elijah not once but twice, commanding him to "…eat, for the journey is too much for you" (1 Kings 19:7-8, NIV). Having refreshed himself, Elijah was ready for the forty-day journey that awaited him.

Our Father does not require that we perpetually ignore basic needs. If we do so, we run perilously close to the sin of pride, believing that we may run the race without fueling ourselves, a thing that only God Himself may do. I have watched many runners over the years attempt to run long distances in the heat without taking the water that is available along any given race event course. Sadly, some have collapsed and required hospital treatment because they would not heed that basic, kindergarten admonition, "if you are thirsty, take a drink." We caregivers sometimes so concern ourselves with our tasks that we forget or make light of the need to take a drink. We are childish only when we ignore God's instruction to fuel up and cool off from time to time.

When pandemonium reigns, slow down and take a drink both from the physical resources God has provided you and from the Well of Living Water. A little cold water goes a long way towards calming the boiling pots. Our Father's Kitchen never closes. You will find, there, a calming peace that will sustain you when the fires glow bright, enabling you to take charge and help both yourself and others to finish well the projects of a day and a lifetime.

Chapter 15

PARTNERING WITH GOD

"He has showed you, O man, what is good. And what does the LORD require of you? To act justly and to love mercy and to walk humbly with your God." Micah 6:8, NIV

"As Jesus was walking beside the Sea of Galilee, He saw two brothers, Simon called Peter and his brother Andrew. They were casting a net into the lake, for they were fishermen. 'Come, follow me,' Jesus said, 'and I will make you fishers of men.' At once they left their nets and followed Him." Matthew 4:18-19, NIV

"I thank my God every time I remember you. In all my prayers for all of you, I always pray with joy because of your partnership in the gospel from the first day until now..." Philippians 1:3, NIV

While taking a stroll around our neighborhood one cool autumn evening, I saw an example of a simple partnership that worked perfectly. A young teenager had decided to take his spaniel for a walk in an unusual way. The dog was tethered by a long leash to the young man who was riding his skateboard, or, rather, being towed on his skateboard by the party-of-the-second-part. Both were having a grand time. Dog-partner got to run full tilt down the street without getting lost or run over, under conditions that dogs surely dream about. He did so using his God-given energies and abilities while being skillfully directed by boy-partner, who kept himself and dog-partner from danger. Boy-partner received a free ride and a chance to sharpen his skateboard skills as he spent time with his canine buddy. It was enough to make anyone chuckle. The arrangement worked because each gave what the other needed in return.

That is a pretty good way to approach a partnership. Each party recognizes what the other does best. Each allows the other the freedom to use his skills and abilities to further the interests of the partnership. Each trusts the other to do his part of the mission. Each receives something of value in return. The best partnerships are both productive and enjoyable. Let's take a closer look at how God works through His partnering with us.

Uncommon Commonality

It's fun being a part of team. If you play softball or bowl or shoot hoops with an intramural team, you know that camaraderie extends beyond wearing the uniform. You are a part of something larger than yourself. Even if it ends with more losses than wins, the season will be remembered for frivolity as well as the fire of the game because being and doing together is what matters.

In Christ, our commonality extends beyond a few months and a limited area of pleasure. It goes deeper than team uniforms and workouts and games. Indeed, our uniforms are invisible, our workouts occur many times daily and the game is one of eternal life and death. We wrestle with our thoughts (Psalm 13:2, NIV), we struggle against visible and invisible wickedness (Ephesians 6:12, NASB), we wage war with heavenly weapons (2 Corinthians 10:4) and we run a marathon-race that will not end for us until life here becomes life hereafter (2 Timothy 4:6-8, NIV). All of us are intimates. We are spiritual members of the fraternity of fatigue and the sorority of sweat. Who and what we share in common will not end, for in the moment of death we will cross a finish line and become victors who swell Heaven's Hall of Fame where we will go on to greater works and glories.

Seize, then, the passion of partnership with Our Father and your fellow teammates. If this all seems, frankly, a bit much to swallow, give yourself some time to take in the surroundings. What say we start by exploring the common bonds that bind our team, our partnership together?

Commonality of Command. In business arrangements, attorneys will often recommend that someone be appointed as a "managing partner" to oversee the day-to-day business operations. As much as we love democracies, there is much to be said for a single captain of the ship. Men will go to great lengths of heroism to serve a commanding officer whom they trust completely. During World War II, Admiral "Bull" Halsey earned a reputation as a tough fighting man but equally as one who greatly valued the men of the rank and file. Two common sailors were discussing that salty old warhorse aboard ship one day. One of them said to the other words to the effect that he was a hard admiral to work for. The other responded, "Yeah, you're right. But I would go to perdition and back for that old goat!" About that time, Admiral Halsey walked around the corner, winked at the second sailor and said "Not so old, son. Not so old!"

Nor does Our Father flinch from Who He Is. We serve the same Ancient of Days whom Daniel beheld in his vision of the four beasts (Daniel 7:9, KJV). He declares about Himself, "*I am* God, and there is no one like Me" (Isaiah 46:9, KJV). And again He proclaims, "I am the Alpha and the Omega…who is and who was and who is to come, the Almighty" (Revelation 1:8, NASB). To Him, all loyalty belongs (Exodus 20:3). That we should love Him with all our heart, soul and mind is, as Jesus explained, the greatest commandment (Matthew 22:37-38). All of us were created by and for Him (Revelation 4:11). In Him is all perfection and He will not give His glory to another (Isaiah 42:8). Only God has accurately foretold from the earliest times what would happen in even the far distant future, "Saying, 'My purpose will be established, And I will accomplish all My good pleasure'" (Isaiah 46:10, NASB).

He is the God of all the heavenly armies, reigning supreme as "The LORD of hosts, He is the King of Glory" (Psalm 24:10, NASB). *Stated another way, Our Father is the God of all conflict and of all crisis.* In his great warrior psalm, David exalts, "Praise be to the LORD my Rock, who trains my hands for war, my fingers for battle. He is my loving God and my fortress, my stronghold and my deliverer, my shield, in whom I take refuge…" (Psalm 144:1-2, NIV). When the mere thought of another ounce of pressure on our already too-tired mind and body is more than we can take, take heart: Jesus, Our Father's direct emissary to us, the exact likeness of His being (Colossians 1:15), has overcome the world (John 16:33). And *that* means that "in all these things we overwhelmingly conquer through Him who loved us" (Romans 8:37, NASB). Where does winning our own battle of conflict and crisis begin? With the One Lord of us all (Ephesians 4:5), He who is our Master Partner.

Commonality of Contract. Law students learn in the opening days of law school the basic elements of a contract. For our purposes, let us summarize them as offer, acceptance and consideration. Someone must offer to do or not do something that has value to each. Both parties must agree to the contract. They must do so having the ability to do so. After all, no one would sell a Mazerrati to a five-year-old. Without the commonality of agreement and obligation, a contract cannot be formed.

When we partner with God, we recognize that He must initiate the relationship. Consider the beginnings of the first contract God had with man. In Genesis, Chapter 12, we find a childless man named Abram to whom God extends an offer. Allow me to paraphrase for a moment. "Get up Abram," God says. "Leave your family roots and neighborhood. Go to a land that I will show you, where I will make a great nation from you and will bless all peoples of the earth through you." Abram, whom God later renamed Abraham, was required to do something to accept the contract. In this case, he was compelled to leave all that was familiar and comfortable and to *trust* God, as his Managing Partner, to show him where to go, and what to do. This "trust," we call faith. It is the constant thread in all God-directed relationships in all ages. Even in secular agreements today we frequently talk about "good faith" in carrying out obligations.

Abraham accepted God's offer by the acts of leaving and going. Some years later, God strengthened the agreement by a profound contractual ceremony in which God personally passed between the required animal sacrifices, signifying His acceptance of the covenant (Genesis 15:17). Likewise, when Moses led the Hebrew children out of Egypt, he ratified God's covenant with the people by blood (Exodus 24:8). The New Covenant recognized that man could never measure up to all of God's holy regulations. Only God could meet all of His requirements. So God *sent* God in the fleshly person of His only begotten son, Jesus Christ, to shed His blood once for all (Hebrews 9:11-28). We share the commonality of a blood partnership through our shared trust-faith in God through Christ, a new covenant in which anyone may participate (2 Peter 3:9). All of us come to Him by faith, for "without faith it is impossible to please God, because anyone who comes to Him must believe that He exists and that He rewards those who earnestly seek Him" (Hebrews 11:6, NIV).

If this seems like dry, heavy going, you may be interested to know that contracts and business agreements are steeped in custom and history. For instance, when a seller of property in 17th century England went to convey title to the buyer, he would take the buyer to the property. There he would hand him a clod of dirt in a process called enfeoffment which completed the title transfer. In the days of Abraham and the Patriarchs, negotiations often took place in front of the local elders and leaders. When Abraham sought land for a burial place for his wife Sarah, he engaged in an interesting dialogue in which he almost certainly overpaid for the property! Yet the agreement is foundational to the relationship. One cannot exist without the other. From the contract flows the oneness. "There is one body and one Spirit, just as you were called in one hope of your calling; one Lord, one faith, one baptism, one God and Father of all who is over all and through all and in all" (Ephesians 4:4-6, NASB). From the oneness flows the life-blood of all that we are here and all that we will be hereafter.

Commonality of Calling and Commitment: Beholding a Masterpiece. Those of us who live in the Dallas-Fort Worth area typically see little of autumn. Most years we seem to go from summer ("we have nine months of warm weather and three months that are pretty darn hot," is how one fella put it) to winter, often in the same day, before returning to warm weather again. This morning is an exception to that rule. Under clear skies, no wind and a waning moon, we received the gift of fall. The air has that crisp, brisk bite that puts extra bounce in your steps. Everywhere you look, there is a coating of white, reflecting God's own light into untold thousands of facets of brilliance. The mist rises from our small local lake where geese line the shore and ducks paddle contentedly through their own reflections on a mirror that is somehow wet. What glory! Yet it pales in comparison to God's greatest masterpiece.

That masterpiece is you. Paul says it this way: "For we are His workmanship, created in Christ Jesus for good works, which God prepared beforehand so that we would walk in them" (Ephesians 2:10, NASB). As beautiful as your favorite autumn scene or work of art may be, it really does not do anything except look pretty. We, however, are works of art designed to function and to function beautifully by doing good deeds that Our Father has prepared for us. As my grandmother used to tell me when I would be standing around while there was work to be done, "Make yourself useful, as well as ornamental!"

I hope you are smiling by now. We are all here for a reason, for many reasons. Some we know, such as raising our children to be godly men and women. Others we may glimpse only from afar. The career that takes so much out of us often leaves us wondering, "What's the use?" In truth, we just do not know the complete answer to many of our questions. But we carry on with our lives, doing the good works as they present themselves, because we know it is the right thing to do. How pleased Our Father must be when we show our commitment to Him even when it does not make much sense to us! No wonder we are called living masterpieces. And, today, our proud Father in Heaven has showcased you for all to see! You are His partner, placed specifically by Him to do what you do best: being a unique person and using your unique set of skills and experiences to help others while advancing the kingdom of heaven. Or, as Peter said long before "WWJD" became the Christian slogan of the day, "For you have been called for this purpose, since Christ also suffered for you, leaving you an example for you to follow in His steps" (1 Peter 2:21, NASB).

Commonality of Culture and Community. Have you ever known of a business where the employees played darts at lunch several times a week? Or what about the clan that never misses a chance for a flag football game when they get together? Or how about a family that hikes in the Rocky Mountains every summer? I like the story of the department boss who would bring doughnuts when morale was down. He called it "attitude adjustment food." Now that's culture we can truly appreciate!

We all need a helping of attitude adjustment from time to time. That is where groups make us all so much better than we would be than if we went it alone. Finding your special place in the Church is not as complicated as you might think but it *is* more important than you can possibly imagine. When I announce long-distance running events, I always tell the runners that what they do matters. Every runner is important because they help others rise to the occasion. Ask any champion level athlete and he will tell you that good competitors make everyone else run better. It is a chain reaction. When you use your time, talent and treasure to get in the game, you push someone else to stay with you stride for stride.

Let me share a story with you. My friend Jimmy and I were competing in a 5K run one hot autumn afternoon some years ago. In that race, we were the best in our age group. At the halfway point, we were next to each other and stayed that way until I managed to find a smidgen of extra energy to edge Jimmy out by a second or so at the finish. Collapsing into the grass, I looked up at him and said, "Jimmy, we were both certified fools for running like that! Next time, let's just flip a coin to see who wins so we don't have to work so hard!" We both had a good laugh, of course. And Jimmy took his revenge on me a number of times. But without Jimmy, I would have been less than what I was capable of being that day.

It works just that way in the Body of Christ. *Those who care, share.* Together, we share Christ (Ephesians 3:6). When we meet, we encourage one another (Hebrews 10:25), using our abilities as we have opportunity to do so. That is why the Church is so important. Those skills do not require that you walk on water or even on ice, for that matter. You need only be you and give yourself. If you like the kitchen, bake for the church ministries. Or if you are a numbers type, good administrators never lack for work. If you are a kid or a kid at heart, smiles and hugs encourage more people to come back to church every week than just about anything else.

We have much more in common with our fellow Christians than with any other group. All of us are "new creatures" (2 Corinthians 5:17, NASB) with whom we share life in our church community. Someday, we will share eternity together. So we have a head start on the getting-to-know-you part of things. When we disagree, we take care of our own problems with one another without resort to legal process (1 Corinthians 6:1-8, Matthew 18:15-17). Why? Because we are family and family always sticks together. Simply by being there, we contribute to the effectiveness of the Church. Our Father will not leave us on the sidelines anytime we want to take a more active role in the fellowship and partnership.

Commonality of Communion. There is not much you can do with a mad dog. You must either get rid of him or get out of his way. You have probably known a few folks who fit the mad-dog rule. No matter what you do, they are always on the attack. It's impossible to have a positive relationship with that kind of person, isn't it?

On the polar extreme, we have those with whom we can share anything, knowing they will hold our hearts with the tenderest of unfailing care. They are more comfortable than old house slippers, more timeless than basic black, more dependable than the tides. Marti teaches the children at school that where relationships are concerned, we all live in a castle with a large moat around it. We alone decide how far to let the drawbridge down with each person who approaches. Those with whom we share the closest communion know the privilege...and responsibility...of the fully open door.

Our Father knows all about castles, drawbridges and mad dogs. With those who are violent, devious and depraved, He shares but little of Himself. *"But He is intimate with the upright"* (Proverbs 3:32, NASB). The import of the word "intimate" suggests a private, secure circle of fellowship that incorporates those who come to Him through Christ. We, dear ones, are His inner circle. He has shared His Word with us, having given us the very Best He has to offer. With us, He is vulnerable. Through us, He seeks to reach those who hurt, those who flee and, yes, even occasionally, those who are the mad dogs. When we are bitten, He heals us. When we cry into our pillow in the night, He comes to us. When we are happy, perplexed or have a case of the ordinaries, Our Father communes with us just as we are.

Commonality of Communication. We speak with Him in prayer. He responds to us through His Holy Spirit and the

Bible. Good partners stay in close touch with one another and especially with the managing partner. Families who can talk about anything, where no subject is taboo, fare better than those where everyone goes their own way. We know these things. Yet what we profess is sometimes distant from our actual practice. Why?

Perhaps it is because our eyeglasses get dirty before we realize it. If you are like me, you probably spend time on a lot of different tasks during the day. I sometimes catch myself staring at the computer screen, trying to get my eyes to focus on something that just isn't clear and I think, "Well, my eyes are just old and tired." Then it dawns on me that I have not cleaned my glasses in a day or two. Pulling them off, I see that they are spotted and smudged, with an assortment of grime that would cause even a garage mechanic to shudder.

I find that I communicate least when I am spotted and smudged before Our Father. Getting off track with the seemingly endless stream of daily business and personal affairs has taken my eyes off the Living Water. When I clean my glasses and splash some cool water in my eyes, I feel and do better. When I stop to spend time with Our Father, my life comes back into focus, with less effort and with greater results.

Commonality of Confession. When I was a child, my mom and her mom had a cottage-type ceramic business. They made various items to order so that the meager proceeds could support their hobby. Having gained a nodding acquaintance with green ware and bisque, glazes and stains, I would sometimes help out. Being rather klutzy, sometimes something would slip out of my hands and break. Always dreading the walk to the workroom, I would sometimes put it off for hours. But then I would go to mom and tell her I had messed up. Not surprisingly, she would give me a hug and tell me everything was OK, sending me back to help again.

Sometimes, the precious treasures of the Kingdom of Heaven slip through our hands and break. When the crash of sin echoes in our ears, we want to run and hide. Many a great person of the Old and New Testament did just that. David said it best: "Whither shall I go from thy spirit or whither shall I flee from thy presence?...If I take the wings of the morning, and dwell in the uttermost parts of the sea, Even there shall thy hand lead me, and thy right hand shall hold me" (Psalm 139: 7, 9-10, KJV). Dear one, go quickly to Him! In the moment you would flee, follow Him instead! How tenderly He deals with us! How extraordinary are His mercies! "If we confess our sins, He is faithful and just to forgive us our sins and purify us from all unrighteousness" (1 John 1:9, NIV). The pot may be broken but the Potter's Hand and wheel turn ever surely. The fall will not keep Him from us. He awaits our approach that He may comfort, heal and prepare us anew for ever more useful work in His kingdom.

Commonality of Comfort. Sometimes, Our Father allows us to be troubled so that when He comforts and communes with us, we will be able to comfort others (2 Corinthians 1:3-5). The fellowship of suffering has, as its flower, the blossom of sweetness that another enjoys. Only spiritual minds may understand this most holy of paradoxes: that we, as imperfect creatures, receive comfort from the suffering of Christ. So it is that in our calluses, bruises and tears, others find refreshment while heaven's garden grows and flourishes. Rejoice! For when your weariness is great, when the load you bear for your family, your church or for a friend is heavy, when you are greatly troubled for the sake of another, far greater still is your reward in the kingdom of heaven.

The Hidden Warrior-Partner

What happens when we lose commonality? In my daily law practice I see it all the time: families have a falling out when a loved one becomes seriously ill or dies, business associates cannot agree on critical issues, a major life crisis befalls someone and in a moment of anger and confusion he engages in conduct that destroys a relationship or a lifetime of good work. At any moment, any of us can fall prey to temporary emotional, spiritual insanity. How do we keep our balance or regain our footing when faced with decaying commonality? In the moment of greatest peril lies the moment of greatest opportunity for the hidden warrior-partner in each of us to emerge.

Gideon's World. Does it seem to you that our society today is not as close-knit as it once was? You may well relate then to Gideon, whose story begins with Chapter 6 of the Old Testament book of Judges. Ominously, the writer of Judges tells us twice that in that time, everyone "did what was right in his own eyes" (Judges 17:6 and 21:25, NASB). Moses had led the Israelites to the Promised Land. His successor, General Joshua, had led the people through the first conquest. After his death, those who had marched with him and those who had seen the mighty miracles God wrought through his hands and those of Moses, also died. "And there arose another generation after them who did not know the Lord, nor yet the work He had done for Israel" (Judges 2:10, NASB).

When the Hebrew children forgot their common bonds, they turned from God. Disaster beget more disaster as Our Father again and again used the surrounding nations to persecute His own so that they would turn back to Him. In essence, that is the story of the period of the Judges (or "leaders," as we might also translate it). Into this vacuum of national leadership, Gideon was born.

We first encounter Gideon threshing out grain in a hidden place so that marauders would not take it. The Midianite enemies were so strong that the Israelites were forced to abandon their homes and live in dens and caves. Few livestock and crops survived. In those days, "the sons of Israel cried to the Lord on account of Midian" (Judges 6:7, NASB). Spiritual decay, economic turmoil, fear, confusion, war and uncertain times all formed a part of Gideon's world just as, in significant measure, they shadow our world today.

Accepting God's Presence and Hearing His Voice. God then appears in a form recognizable to Gideon. Notice the greeting: "The Lord is with you, O valiant warrior" (Judges 6:12, NASB). How strange! Gideon is *hiding*– out of necessity, certainly, but Gideon is decidedly *not* the image of a man of war. *God sees in us what others do not yet see.* In the young shepherd boy David, God saw the future King of Israel and the head of the lineage from which the Christ would be born (1 Samuel 16:7, 11-13). He, alone, sees the perfect leader-partner that sleeps within us. Have you ever, in a sudden emergency or under adverse conditions, found yourself doing something you never thought you could do? Maybe you comforted a child who had lost a family member, or you rendered aid at an accident scene, or you picked up pieces of someone's home, broken by a violent storm, or picked up pieces of someone's heart, broken by violence of a different sort, and helped repair it. By the lessons of conflict and crisis, Our Father prepares you for the hour and for the events in which He will reveal to others that you are His chosen one for the task at hand.

In these latter days, Our Father speaks to us in ways that are appropriate to the point in time in which we live. He is always consistent with Himself. What God proclaims through the Bible stands supreme. Do not be deceived. You will never hear His voice leading you in a direction that runs counter to the Word He has proclaimed in Scripture (see Galatians 1:8, NASB, where Paul emphatically declares that "even if we, or an angel from heaven, should preach to you a gospel contrary to what we have preached to you, he is to be accursed!"). Our first point of reference for His voice in our life is the Bible. Tuck its words away into your heart. Meditate upon them. Absorb their meaning, layer by layer. Let your daily experiences call to mind what you have read and thought about. When times of drought come, when all is dark around you, you will "be like a tree firmly planted by streams of water, which yields its fruit in its season… and in whatever he does, he prospers" (Psalm 1:3, NASB). So is the one who delights himself in God's Word.

Our Father will also use others to show us His way. "But in abundance of counselors there is victory" (Proverbs 11:15, NASB). Heed the wisdom of those who know you well and whose hearts are, like yours, devoted to His higher calling. Stay in close touch with those mighty prayer warriors who are ever ready to seek God's will, with you and for you at any hour. Consider the voices of family, loved ones, friends and colleagues, filtering all through the light of the revealed truth of Scripture. Know that Our Father can use strangers and familiar faces alike to lead you in the path you should go. Wait expectantly for the puzzle pieces to come together, as they surely will, in God's good time.

We have the Helper dwelling within us. His name is that of the blessed Third Member of the Trinity: the Holy Spirit. When Jesus shared His last meal with the disciples on the night of His betrayal, Jesus explained that the Father would send a "Helper" who would live with them forever (John 14:16, NASB). He is sometimes called the "Counselor" or the "Comforter." Your church tradition may refer to Him as the "Paraclete," which is the literal rendering of the Greek word *parakletos* that is translated in many beautiful ways. The idea is that of an advocate, someone to plead one's cause, someone to help, aid and assist us now that Jesus is physically absent from the earth. The Holy Spirit perfectly represents us before Our Father in Heaven. Note how Paul says it: "…the Spirit helps us in our weakness… the Spirit Himself intercedes for us with groans that words cannot express" (Romans 8:26, NIV). This very same Helper works to show you God's will (Romans 8:27).

In the silence of the tender moment, Our Father plucks our heart strings. "Be still, and know that I am God" (Psalm 46:10, NIV) was spoken to all who yearn for His Holy Presence. Like children seeking the company of a wise parent or grandparent, we turn to Him in prayer. "Pray without ceasing" (1 Thessalonians 5:17, NASB) means that we speak with Him often during the day and night.

A whispered word of love to Him when we wake in the night, an expression of awe at the mysteries and miracles of life, a brief request for the one in need, all please Him and comfort us in the bargain. When we do so, we are telling Him that He is real and personal to us in the here and now.

And so Gideon faced the choice we all face at some point in our journey. He could have said, "I don't know who you are, but you have the wrong man!" Or he could have talked it through with God, just as he did. When we, like Gideon, accept the active, near presence of Our God and Father, all of His wondrous ways lie open to us. "But with God, all things are possible" (Matthew 19:26, NIV). He can even make a warrior out of a timid farmer. Because it pleases Him to use common clay for noble purposes, any of us can be called for His special duty, beyond the normal affairs of our day, at any time.

Accepting God's Command. It is one thing to hear God but quite another to walk into unknown territory based solely upon His command, one that sometimes makes little sense to us. Active faith allows His words, "Go in this your strength…Have I not sent you?" (Judges 6:14, NASB), to reach fertile soil within our soul. As it was with Gideon, so it is with all who would follow our Lord to higher ground.

Our Father understands and accepts our questions when they are asked sincerely and in humility. When Gideon asked how the Lord could be with him when enemies were destroying his country, God did not *condemn*, but, rather, *commanded* Gideon to go and deliver Israel from the hands of the Midianites because He had selected

Gideon for that specific purpose. After that, Gideon's questions addressed practicalities. How was Gideon to do the job God was sending him to do? Gideon was an unknown. His family was not an important one and Gideon himself was the youngest in his family, in a culture where the oldest son from a respected clan might be expected to lead. Obscurity poses no problem to Our Father. Those whom He calls, He equips. In one sentence, God assures Gideon, "Surely I will be with you, and you shall defeat Midian as one man." For Gideon, that was enough.

In trial practice, skilled attorneys seem to have an instinct when to stop asking questions. Great attorneys have a mortal fear of asking one question too many, lest a witness ruin a carefully laid plan with a bad response. God's children, also, should cultivate a healthy fear of asking Him one question too many, particularly when we know what He desires from us. Sometimes He blesses obedience with uncommon blessings. Just ask Gideon. In less than one minute (read Judges 6:12-16 out loud for yourself and time it), Gideon went from scared farmer to Commanding General. It has to be a record for the fastest promotion in history! Sometimes, we need only say "Yes, Lord" for Him to work as effectively in us as He did with Gideon.

How did Gideon respond to God's commission? By asking that He accept an offering. In the culture of the day, hospitality meant peace. If a man ate a meal with you, you either were already friends or you became friends when the hospitality and meal were accepted. Gideon knew this. If God had really called him, so Gideon must have reasoned, God would accept his food offering as a sign that confirmed the commission. Having presented the meal to the Divine Visitor, Gideon did not have to wait for an an-swer. With a flash of fire, God consumed the offering and then vanished from Gideon's sight.

The principle for us today is the same. If you are indeed called to a particular task, God will honor His work through you, accepting the sacrifice of your time, talent and treas-ure as you offer it. Do not expect Him to appear with fire from Heaven but do expect that He will touch your heart in a way that you will clearly understand as He confirms you in the purpose to which you are called. "Peace to you, do not fear" (Judges 6:23, NASB). It is God's message to sin-ful but redeemed man throughout the ages. The angels spoke it to those shepherds who first heard the glad tid-ings of Messiah's birth on the lonely plains of Bethlehem. "Fear not," said the angel of the Lord, "for, behold, I bring you good tidings of great joy that shall be unto all peo-ple…Glory to God in the highest, and on earth, peace, good will toward men" (Luke 2:10, 14, KJV). Those who accept Him through Christ have His favor, forever.

Accepting God's Plan. Be prepared for the unortho-dox, for God is never limited by what we think He should do! First, He tested Gideon's commitment to Himself. The order was a plain one: take two of his father's bulls, pull down the altar of the false god Baal, cut down the infa-mous Asherah pole next to it, and build a proper altar to God, sacrificing the bulls and using the wood of the Asherah pole for fuel. Talk about an attention grabber! Nothing could more publicly proclaim Gideon's sincerity in following God than this. And it would require basic lead-ership to show Israel that he had the courage to tackle a tough job.

Courage. Where does it come from? Someone has said that in a great battle, a sensible man would run away. In Gideon's case, courage found its genesis in devotion to God. Casting care for himself aside, Gideon swallowed hard (several times, probably!), enlisted the help of ten servants and did all that God commanded. Gideon still had fear—he did his work at night "because he was too afraid of his father's household and the men of the city to do it by day" (Judges 6:27, NASB) —but He went forward anyway.

Gideon's obedience made all the difference. When daylight came, of course everyone learned quickly what had happened. It did not take long to find out that Gideon had sold out to the old God even though they had adopted a new god. They wanted his head, literally. Moral decisions, decisions of great truth and occasion, require a hard choice, one filled with consequences. Gideon did not know for certain if he would die or not that day. But he did not look back. Like Moses who left Egypt in the rearview mirror, for Gideon the land of known security no longer attracted him, for he had found the warrior within.

Make the hard decision based on God's definition of integrity and you will not look back, wondering what might have been. Keep yourself pure for God and He will be intimate with you (Proverbs 3:32). Grab yourself by the bootstraps *in the strength that you have* and God will multiply it exponentially. Each time, He will call you to still greater battles. Expect testing and rejoice in the lessons learned, for you are becoming more like Him every day. All the while, you will be growing in those fruits of the Spirit ("love, joy, peace, patience, kindness, goodness, faithfulness, gentleness, and self-control," Galatians 5:22-23, NIV) that mark you as one who has gone on to maturity in Christ (Hebrews 6:1, NIV).

Having tested Gideon's commitment and courage, God entrusted Gideon with more of His plan. When Gideon called for warriors, they came because Gideon had shown himself to be approved by God. Likewise, when by your deeds you stand for that which matters in God's eyes, others will see it and will listen to you when you speak. Ask yourself the question, "When someone speaks about Christ, am I more apt to listen to him if I know he is living a life consistent with what Jesus taught?" Go then and live accordingly, for a partner is known by how he behaves towards all that the partnership honors.

When God was ready to defeat the enemies of Israel through Gideon, God took his chosen partner aside and said, "The people who are with you are too many for me to give Midian into their hands, for Israel would become boastful, saying, 'My own power has delivered me'" (Judges 7:2, NASB). Our Sovereign God directs victory so that all will see Him and know that He Is God. Gideon obeyed when God narrowed the forces from 32,000 to 10,000 to 300, but with what fears and misgivings we can only wonder. Consider the odds. The opposing forces were "as numerous as locusts; and their camels were without number, as numerous as the sand on the seashore" (Judges 7:12, NASB). Any commander faced with such odds would be afraid. And Gideon was. So Our Father took Gideon by the hand and showed him through the eyes of two enemy soldiers that they knew God was against them because of a dream He sent.

Be sure to catch what happened next: "It came about when Gideon heard the account of the dream and its interpretation, that he bowed in worship" (Judges 7:15, NASB). Do you wonder, sometimes, whether saying grace before a meal or offering thanks at the close of a day or saying the short silent prayer of gratitude matters to Him? Here is your answer! Our Father inserted that sentence to reassure you that all His warriors worship, sometimes when it is most unlikely. Say "Thank You, Father," when that SUV which cannot see you in its blind spot does not hit you. Bless His Name for ears that hear the meadowlark and eyes that behold the faces of our loved ones. Praise Him for the majesty of all His creation. Praise Him for the small work, well performed, that you complete in His name this day. Worship Him in the life you live, the thoughts you think, the hopes and dreams that are uniquely yours. When you do, you are a Gideon, honoring Our Father at the battle line.

Oh, what unseen forces are at work constantly in the heavenly realms on our behalf! The battle we so dread, the test that so unnerves us, the foe who so frightens us all are as clay in the Potter's Hands! As Daniel said, "He sets up kings and deposes them. He gives wisdom to the wise and knowledge to the discerning. He reveals deep and hidden things; He knows what lies in darkness, and light dwells with Him" (Daniel 2:21-22, NIV). He "lets the nations know they are but men" (Psalm 9:20, NIV). This One is *Our God and Our Father*! Who, then, shall we fear?

That night, God threw all the enemy into a panic after Gideon and his 300 smashed their pitchers, exposed their torches and stood their ground. They never lifted a sword (if they even had one!), never suffered a wound, while all around them The Lord God of Hosts caused the enemy to kill one another. God's plan, God's way, God's time, God's partner doing the impossible with ease. That is you, there, with Him.

Passionate About Partnership

Relationship is the living fabric of life. The fabled emperor who had no clothes became so caught up in the greed for grander, costlier fabric that he ultimately failed to realize he was naked. Without healthy relationships, though we be arrayed as kings, we are in reality garbed with the poorest of rags. Our Father longs to place the robe of royalty about our shoulders, just as Jesus taught in the story of the Prodigal Son. We are children of the King! As David, Israel's King, celebrated with unrestrained, joyous dancing when the Ark of the Covenant came to Jerusalem, let us in like fashion be unashamed to passionately embrace all that He Is so that our partnership with Him may bear more fruit.

One Operating System. "This is my Father's World," the old hymn exalts. "Though the wrong seems oft so strong, God is the ruler yet!" Your computer runs on only one operating system. The Partnership is no different. The parts are not interchangeable with the junk of the world. We are His and we operate by His system.

One Reward. Are we partners or just hired hands? Partners share in the ultimate success of the enterprise. Each partner devotes his *best* time and efforts to ensure that the outcome meets partnership expectations. So we suffer some ill will, build up a few spiritual calluses and aches in our hearts over the very world that laughs at us. Why? Because we *are* different. Because we *are* His. Because we *know* that His life-blood is in the business to which we have been called as partners. "The wages of sin is death; but the gift of God is eternal life through Jesus Christ Our Lord" (Romans 6:23, KJV). Let others work for peanuts. As a partner, you have far greater rewards awaiting you (1 Corinthians 2:9).

Location, Location? Our Father can use us anywhere for His purpose, anytime. But that does not mean we should risk our spiritual safety for commercial gain. Recall the story of Abraham's nephew, Lot, who went with Abraham when God called him to leave his land and family. As God prospered Abraham, so, too, Lot prospered. Finally, they had to split up because there was not enough pasture and water to accommodate Abraham's and Lot's flocks and herds at the same time. Abraham allowed Lot to choose first which direction to go. "So Lot chose for himself all the valley of the Jordan" (Genesis 13:11, NASB) and ultimately settled in the beautiful, yet hideously evil, town of Sodom (Genesis 19:1). Lot remained true to the Lord but it cost him his home, his possessions and his wife. Do not do as Lot did. Keep this instruction in mind: "Do not be bound together with unbelievers; for what partnership has righteousness and lawlessness, or what fellowship has light with darkness?" (2 Corinthians 6:14, NASB). Choose the location closest to the path of righteousness and you will honor God while preserving your heart and home.

Trigger Buttons and Getting Back on the Bicycle. In every successful relationship, the parties have an understanding of what really angers the other person. God is no different. Look closely at His trigger buttons: "There are six things the Lord hates, seven that are detestable to Him: haughty eyes, a lying tongue, hands that shed innocent blood, a heart that devises wicked schemes, feet that are quick to rush into evil, a false witness who pours out lies and a man who stirs up dissension among brothers" (Proverbs 6:16-19, NIV). Dig deeper with me, please. Our Father hates pride, the "me" before the "He." Some believe that all sin starts with pride because it dethrones God from our lives. Pride begets lies, which give way to evil plans, evil deeds, and evil conversation about others. When the ragweed of mischief fully opens, it sows strife and rebellion among the partnership.

When we do what we want without regard to Our Father's will, we fracture the partnership. That is why it is so very important to come often before Him to say, "I was wrong. Please get me back on track." Note the promise: "If we confess our sins, He is faithful and just to forgive us our sins and to cleanse us from all unrighteousness" (1 John 1:9, NASB). It hurts when we fall off the bicycle. The sooner we get back on, the sooner the pain will go away. It is one of the most essential practices of the successful Christian partner. Quickly go to Him and quickly return to your rightful place by His side.

Blessing Follows Service. Not all rewards and blessings are the same but they all flow from the same Father. Our trust in Him must necessarily extend to the end of all that will happen to us in this life. Faith's Hall of Fame encompasses the mighty and the minions alike, for no act of service is too small for Him to notice. After all, even the cold cup of water given in His name has its reward (Matthew 10:42).

Virtue may, indeed, be its own reward as our forefathers have taught us. Yet Our Father takes such delight in us that sometimes our service, rendered faithfully to others, becomes a gift to ourselves. When Marti and I began the process of becoming foster parents, I had to tough out much of it. The paperwork is highly personal, even invasive. We were, correctly I might add, subjected to a background check more rigorous than that required of entrants to a well-known national law enforcement organization. Some of the rules and regulations require a significant adjustment of our personal space and daily habits while others make little sense at all. At any hour of the day or night your phone may ring with the inquiry whether you can accept one or more children in severe distress, about whom you know almost nothing. If you accept them, you also accept the often extreme problems with which they are burdened. They become *your* burdens and you do not put them down until the children move to another setting. Whether any of the countless hours of work you have placed into a given child will ever yield fruit, you are seldom, if ever, privileged to know. You are under constant review and undergo a number of hours of continuing education each year. As a foster parent, you either accept all of this and much, much more or you quit, plain and simple.

Ministry, generally, is like that. But sometimes Our Father delightedly throws in a perquisite (or "perk," as most of us call it) that becomes a fountainhead of joy unspeakable. In our case, it led to the adoption of our dear daughter Felicity and the opening of some of the greatest moments I will ever know. Who could have foreseen such an outcome that first time we went to a foster parent training class? Our Father could and did. I believe passionately He will reward your service beyond anything that you, too, can imagine.

Not All Partnerships Are Created Equal. One word of warning: not all partnerships are worth the investment. We recognize that it is customary in some business environments for particularly talented, dedicated and "acceptable" individuals to be made partners in the organization. How many times have you seen news headlines about partners being tied to civil or criminal liability for some act or series of acts attributed jointly to the partners? The world system offers the opportunity for great folly under the guise of "partnership." Accept no moral, legal or financial compromises from those with whom you join hands. Disaster awaits those who fail to perform initial and ongoing due diligence in partnership affairs, as any reputable business attorney will counsel you. If Jesus instructed His disciples that He was sending them out "like sheep among wolves. Therefore be as shrewd as snakes and as innocent as doves" (Matthew 10:16, NIV), should we be any less on our guard in all of our stewardship relations?

Concluding Thought: It's supposed to be Fun. Our Father equips us with wondrously unique talents and experiences so that we fit exactly into place in His perfect plan. It is not all pain and no gain. In fact, it is supposed to be fun. Think back to our boy and dog story. When we allow Him to take us for the ride of our lives, we can expect to work up a sweat. But Oh! What a glorious time we will have, now and throughout eternity!

Chapter 16

SAVORING THE MOMENT

"To every thing there is a season, and a time to every purpose under the heaven" Ecclesiastes 3:1, KJV

If variety is the spice of life, it is a wonder that most of us don't have indigestion. Perhaps it is an occupational hazard of life in the 21st century, but something about it feels undeniably over the top, like a dessert that has too many confectionery layers to be pleasantly edible. Sometimes I wonder if people, like great food, are best savored in smaller bites.

I am glad to see that home construction is returning to the use of outdoor living space that is visible to others. Front porches and open back yards invite neighbors to stop and chat. Marti and I have recently moved to an established neighborhood where our back yard opens onto a small lake ("pond" is a better word but, being Texans, we are prone to exaggeration) that has a walking path around it. Aside from the community of ducks that have adopted us due, no doubt, to our generosity with the feed sack, we have already enjoyed many happy hours communing with the locals. Over time, I hope our window on the world becomes hopelessly overcrowded with neighbors whose friendship we intend to savor. When all life seems lunatic, we may still enjoy countless special moments that will help us adjust to the stresses and changes of the nano-speed journey of this present age.

How I pray that we all grasp the beauty of the moments with which we are blessed! How sad it is for life to wing by us, leaving us only with a few feathers and no recollection of the meadow lark's song! As I mature and age, I find that my interest in the small things has increased. What wonders does a mere square foot of my front lawn contain? How do our grandchildren play? Where do the local ducks go for the winter? Who is that young man playing the jazzy saxophone in the park? Why do colors seem to have an unending variety of shades?

Moments matter. They matter more than the sum of the days and years that now tell me I am a veteran of many, many conflicts and crises. As I count the purposes under heaven, I want to slow down the seasons, holding on to each summer hummingbird vision, each pecan-autumn moon for more than an eye blink. And I want to know each of you who with whom I have walked these pages.

Savoring the moment requires that we see life as a gift, no matter how many pots may be boiling over. There is no original thinking in that one, is there? The trick is not in smelling the blossom but in remembering the exact fragrance when winter winds beckon us to put another log on the fire. Can you recall the taste of summer watermelon, both hot and cold? Does your ear retain the sound of your children's voices when they were four, eight, fourteen and eighteen years old? What did your first home or special room smell like? If you remember any of these, you are blessed with an extraordinary perception, for you have grasped the simple, timeless moment.

Savoring the moment means opening our eyes to God. Again, forget about original thinking. Our Father creates every day, everywhere a world of uncontained delight. Have you ever considered a full moon through winter-bare tree branches or a single beached shell? What can we say to the cry of the goose, the cacophony of sound that is a college football bowl game, the sense-assaulting fragrances of a county fair, or the kaleidoscopic colors of a crowded shopping mall near Christmastime? To see Our Father equally in the cold fog of a San Francisco morning and the texture of sand between waves on a Galveston beach—there lies vision and glory.

Savoring the moment means accepting that what the moment brings is unique and will pass in due haste. If it brings the ordinary affairs of the day, they have their special place for we will remember our daily routines as a slice of who we were at a particular time. If it brings tears, let them have their way, for they show that we are made to feel life as well as to observe it. If the moment brings confusion, rejoice that we have much to learn. If it brings sweat and toil then grasp the peasant pleasure of honest work. If it brings sleep, reflect that even there God is with us.

Savoring the moment means that we have acquired the spiritual gift of being able to be content in that moment. From each moment, we learn something of what it is to be content in other moments from which we, in turn, learn that contentment may be found in any moment where we seek the company of Our Father and our Jesus. When we know Their Presence, we know that neither eternity nor any conflict or crisis can separate us from "the love of God that is in Christ Jesus our Lord" (Romans 8:38, NIV). *Savoring the moment means that we have learned how to constructively work through conflict and crisis.*

Being something of a student of poetry since my youth, I sometimes lean on verse to express a point for which I have an inadequate vocabulary. Please indulge me one last time. Marti found the following poem that is attributed to the mid-nineteenth century poet Mary Ann Evans, who used the male penname of George Eliot. It goes like this:

Two lovers by a moss-grown spring;
They leaned soft cheeks together there,
Mingled the dark and sunny hair,
And heard the wooing thrushes sing.
O budding time!
O love's blest prime!

Two wedded from the portal stept:
The bells made happy carolings,
The air was soft as fanning wings,
White petals on the pathway slept.
O pure-eyed bride!
O tender pride!

Two faces o'er a cradle bent:
Two hands above the head were locked:
These pressed each other while they rocked,
Those watched a life that love had sent.
O solemn hour!
O hidden power!

Two parents by the evening fire:
The red light fell about their knees
On heads that rose by slow degrees
Like buds upon the lily spire.
O patient life!
O tender strife!

The two still sat together there,
The red light shone about their knees;
But all the heads by slow degrees
Had gone and left the lonely pair.
O voyage fast!
O vanished past!

The red light shone upon the floor
And made the space between them wide;
They drew their chairs up side by side,
Their pale cheeks joined, and said, "Once more!"
O memories!
O past that is!

What tender strife Our Father uses to grow us into His perfect one! How soon the conflict and crisis that so concerns us fades into the mystery of eternity! Gather rosebuds while you may for fast goes the voyage. Bless Our Father, bless most holy Jesus for the gift of great struggle, for in it you find yourself as surely as you see His hand directing you to a past, a present and a future that is your forever tapestry. May you find each of His gifts that await you in your times of conflict and crisis.